As we focus on space travel and wormholes, we seem to

dismiss that we ourselves are portals,

vessels, somewhat empty yet receptive cups that we can fill with

God's love and guidance, or not.

I do not know if we will ever receive a universal explanation,

other than what is written on our hearts, but we cannot deny

that happiness is a state of mind and being.

The world is rapidly changing, or is it the people? It seems that

Mother Nature is being taken for granted, for we are shifting

from Oak and Water to Smoke and Fire.

We are God's portals

Through Free Will we are bestowed the choice

To follow the way of Truth, or the way of Ignorance.

-Portals(1927), John Azoth's Collection of Poems

We are running out of time… My name is Zeal, the reason I write to you is for the preservation of Love, Truth, and Hope. For we are approaching a time of darkness, and no one can be sure what will slip through this storm… Depending on how long this has been buried in the dust or if it even made it through, allow me to paint a picture of the time:

I live in a little house, but just big enough for myself, mom, little brother, and stepfather who is still living with us in order to make things 'economically easier'.

I basically started to drift away from the deep mother-son connection with mom once I started to get older and more in-tune with myself. Don't get me wrong, I love and respect my mother, but not having transparency or the ability to relate emotionally or think on the same wavelength with one's mother can lead to a lot of suppressed rage and frustration. On the other hand, my little sister Lex and brother (half-brother if you want to get technical, different daddies) Grady, are rays of sunlight that pierces right through the frequent dark cloud that hovers over our home life, a small diamond shrouded by coal.

Moving on from the fluff, I have always seemed to be a drifter, a wandering soul; blending in from crowd to crowd, changing faces whenever seemingly necessary. Really, I just wanted to be surrounded by people and never be that 'alone' weird kid. One aspect of being alone that I enjoyed, however, was reading and shortly after, writing. If I found material that I was interested in... game over. No one could separate me from the simple magic of the page; visualizing the interactions and dialogue, the development of the broken hero... a manifested world created in order to inspire thought and imagination. This was my escape, my heaven that I couldn't really understand or explain completely but could never question its authenticity.

An issue with growing up in a progressive and technologically driven society with aims to cause as little work and mental effort for the human being as possible, is that interest in books and the value of the written word isn't cultivated as much into our youth. Learning is 'processed' through online simulations and programs that are pre-dominantly 'voice taught'(pre-recorded or AI operated through the use of algorithms) meaning there is little actual reading or interaction involved between students and their teachers.

Books and works of art have become digitized, eliminating paper almost completely from the market and causing the few

remaining pieces to be carelessly destroyed or cheaply pawned. A great divide is present where art, renaissance, and beauty have become arbitrary and a fading memory. The news justifies that this rift has been beneficial for the environment, however, people with common sense and a grasp of reality can see otherwise. The amount of air pollution and dumping has tripled since 2022 (currently 2033), as well as the chemical run-off from the copious large factories around the world, leading to the death of little over 40% of marine life. Our vegetation has taken a toll on both land and sea and mother nature has no choice but to purge the toxins. This whole ordeal of 'switching' to artificial intelligence and digital living was foreseen, even planned, but the public has grown too comfortable and ignorant to even notice it all happening… Many of us seem to make an unconscious choice to keep our ears plugged at some point, but we must not give up hope and we must gain awareness. It's amazing how quickly perspectives and values can change once the cards have been shuffled overnight, which is why I stick closely to the law of Neutrality, to not overcommit towards any certain belief or line of thought, aka remaining objective in this emotionally paranoid time. It is a value that has helped keep me grounded over this period of mania. However, there is something about the symbolism of the bible and other sacred texts, particularly esoteric Christianity, or old Gnosticism, which is derived from *Gnosis,* or inner knowing and conscious awareness of spiritual truth, guarded from the profane by the ancient mystic Christians throughout the ages, that draws me into a feeling of devotion and piety. It seems that many 'atheists' today revert to atheism due to the overbearing and offensive bloodthirst of many organized religions of today. The preacher who beckons to 'save' people, yet that very preacher is cheating on his wife with another church-going woman who is married to another church-going man. A new form of holy corruption.

There is a scattering of information through the world, with Truth mixed in with the lies and folly, causing the upcoming generations to be lost and left to the winds of change and confusion. I have become thirsty for true wisdom and 'gnosis' and the lies begin to sit bitterly on my tongue and ears. This abrupt change in viewpoint has lost me a decent number of friends because I won't submit to the common beliefs or willingly remain in ignorant blissful sleep, which in turn aren't true friends to begin with. Granted, there are core sets of values that we all hold as a human race that separate us from the beasts. Don't we?

This decision was difficult but necessary in order to break free from the mental jail cell which I was guided into through clinging onto old beliefs and institutions. So, why are things so critical now? Thanks for asking! There seems to be another subtle split taking place within the world, a split between the human soul and the body, or perhaps a spiritual test? As I grew up saturated in the world around me, I started to experience the feeling that my thoughts weren't always my own or caused by my own psyche alone. Much like the typical 'looney' story, I thought this was normal and that everyone thought like this. I just kept going about my life as a cheerful lad. Not too much sooner my reading obsession naturally shifted into a writing obsession, creating my own worlds and experiences, not having to conform to the systems of others. Freedom.

It was quite a breaking point as I was truly able to enter a state of mental and emotional flow that I have never experienced before or thought possible. However, this literary current carried me into deep emotional reservoirs that were completely foreign to my nurturing but confused and rigid family background. The thought of 'letting go', whatever that meant, seemed like something terrifying and destructive, but at the same time seemed to be the only thing that was holding me back from my true potential as an expression of my true self, whatever that was. This path leads to a mental tug-of-war for a big chunk of my life, torn between a world of materialism and ignorant bliss, or living as a lone wolf who stays true to his Nature and Higher Purpose. Is there a way to find a balance? To my surprise, the big picture was way bigger than me, for there are many lone wolves like me who have come here to initiate the revolution of the soul through different art forms (music, film, painting, writing, singing, etc.). These wanderers heard the call of trapped souls and oppression and couldn't resist the opportunity, the call to Love.

It feels like a form of assignment, to come here, to forget, to experience, to remember. Our own personal Quest for the Grail of self-understanding. There is many embarking on this journey of life, including you and I, but in one form or another, the wool of illusion and lies is still over the eyes of the many sheep(us). This is a risk we are all willing to take in order to fulfill the duty and honor of the Infinite Love. One of the many beauties of Earth is that she can support all kinds of energetic backgrounds and signatures, most of these energies or frequencies are invisible to the human eye. Within all of us there is DNA that lays dormant (sleeping) and inactive, this has been concealed and completed on purpose over generations (poisonous food and water as well as toxins/heavy metals within the air through 'Chem-Trails') by a small group of control-hungry tyrants backed by corporate machines for us to keep coming back here to work for them and remain bound to the material and the non-important. But more importantly, the negative thoughts that have become commonplace in the collective mindset of the People, which has given birth to a general discomfort and the feeling that 'something isn't quite right'.

Everyone has different latent abilities that make up their own unique organism, just like how everyone has a different fingerprint or genetic code, in order to represent their own mark and representation in the universe, all of us creating a

symphony of Life. The poisons in our air and in many of our

foods are sneaky ways to keep these latent abilities in their

slumber and tucked away until we snap out of it. Let us hope

that we can all come to our senses in time…

The Beginning

Not long ago, in a galaxy not so far away, there was a Light.

Not particularly special, but bright.

This Light had spread over time, inevitably, like water being

poured into an empty cup, illuminating the basin of dark space.

This Light's brother was Dark, for without each other, they

would not exist…

Their father was Creation, the glue of all existence, and the brothers Light and Dark competed for his Love.

They still fight today, but the thing is, they use us humans as leverage against each other.

The only issue, however, is that Father gave us humans the Free Will, in order to make the choice for ourselves, causing Light and Dark to continue their ongoing competition, not knowing that Creation loves them both, unconditionally.

-S.M. Guy

October 14th, 2014

I woke up, gasping for air, rising from my bed like Frankenstein when he was shocked to life. It was another journey, a trip into the dream realm which involved a goddess of a woman who seems to appear to me when I need something… an idea. Dreya, I called her. This trip was like most of the others; ending in confusion and bags the size of Texas under my eyes. "Where the hell was I?" was a frequent thought that came to me during mornings like these, "Does it mean anything?". Paranoia strikes early as I cycle through the possibilities.

I walk into the bathroom that I share with my little brother, and I turn the knob all the way as cold as the water could possibly go. I watched the water run for a little bit, wondering what it would be like to be water; flowing, careless, balancing and evening out, then going down the drain in a steady vortex in order to begin a whole new cycle. I then gave myself a good splash, rubbing my eyebrows and the soft skin on my temples. I dried my face off, gradually emerging back into reality. I was going to school for Psychology at the time so I could understand the puzzle of the mind and the unconscious mind specifically, in order to help people through the murky dark waters of the unknown self, the shadow self. But the underlying truth, was that I wanted to understand myself, which is a true mystery to many of us. The American education system as it is, however, isn't really in my 'best interest' since it is a corrupt system that I was already duped into as a child. With that being written, I have been self-educating the old-fashioned way through a cocktail of research through books, internet videos, and a whole lot of self-reflection on experiences that have assisted in molding me into what I am becoming.

I have been driven to a point where meditation and introspection have been the only effective ways to calm all of the noise of scattered thoughts and misguided emotions that my brain gets bombarded with. The idea and label of the word 'meditation' seems to have been tabooed or exiled in modern times, maybe it is time to give an updated explanation, or at least what meditation is to me:

There is the traditional method of sitting still and letting the thoughts (negative or positive, or both) wash over you and consciously guide these thoughts, like a shepherd, to a safe, nurturing middle-ground (Earth, or Midgard in Nordic mythology. Hence the term 'down-to-Earth') of the Mind and Heart. In this age of noise and distraction, however, this simple practice has become less realistic for people. I have found that we do not have to sit completely still in lotus position and close our eyes and force ourselves, but through Contemplative Activity forms such as walking, biking, reading, and even talking with someone close to your heart and who you trust can all guide one into a calm meditative state. Often-times I doubt myself and my ability, mostly due to lack of focus and motivation, it can be a hard pill to swallow telling the truth to yourself. I walked into the kitchen to make a cup of coffee, the Earthly Resurrector. I try not to drink too much of the stuff, but I've grown to be quite fond of a good espresso. As I let the brew cool off, my routine lately has been to look through the sliding glass window parallel to the kitchen which provides a wide view of the lush South Florida vegetation (mostly palm trees and neatly trimmed hedges) that form a barrier between the houses and the canal that ran through the neighborhood. Recently, there has been this Blue-jay that seems to exchange eerily understanding glances with me through the glass while it splashes in the limestone bird bath outside of the window. I have never seen such a beautiful bird in my life; the way the feathers are slicked back on the top of the head, as if it were the Frank Sinatra of birds, the gorgeous blue and black feathers with a belly of white that bounces joyfully as they go about their business. My buddy has been making an appearance for the past week, only a brief gaze of recognition necessary in order to catch up with each other. Birds are quite fascinating.

The schedule for the day was going to consist of me going to my close friend Crow's house and spending the day 'productively' in a haze of THC, electronic music, and laughs. What can beat that? It was another sunny south Florida day, being from Michigan originally, the coldest day in Florida is still considered paradise to people residing in the 'mitten'(refer to a map of Michigan in order to understand the reference). Also, being in high school, the list of responsibilities included: eating, sleeping, school, and sports (Ice hockey and Lacrosse) so I basically spent all my free time not caring and making, as well as forgetting, memories with 'friends'.

My best friend at the time, Joe, was still in Michigan with the rest of the gang and was way too high-spirited to be mixed in with the dull northern crew. We became friends in elementary school and were best buds ever since. Something I found out recently about Joe is that he is highly psychic and empathic, meaning that he can take on the thought waves and emotions of others (often without warning or invitation), which is possibly what we recognized in each other, unconsciously, as young lads. We tried to keep contact as often as motivated, but as you can imagine, distance and new beginnings can leave old relationships on standby and eventually they organically fade away as a pleasant (or not so pleasant) memory.

I began to adjust to this place well enough; the beautiful, warm, slow vibes... content vibes. Life seems to pass at a calmer, more relaxed pace than in Michigan (depends on where) due to South Florida being a big retirement spot. The reasoning behind my family migration consists of my dad getting laid off by his job due to the U.S. economy crash of 2008. There have been men and women in high financial and political arenas who are corrupted by power and wealth and play with the inflation rates and currency or entire countries, like a big Monopoly game.

Unfortunately for the people(us) who live these games out, it isn't such a funny power game. Pops is a very smart man, but stubborn and traditional, making outside-the-box thinking seem very foreign and unrealistic when it comes to the next step. However, he was able to get into contact with an old roller skating (yes, my dad roller skated) friend who was selling contracts in a new and promising silver mine being built in Mexico, which sounds pretty sketchy in hindsight, but this goes back to the desperation and 'fresh start' that father was yearning for. Since he was freshly divorced, I am sure South Florida appeared as a beacon of hope. Just like Crow's nest was my beacon of escape.

The main issue with the silver mine gig was that we all had to wait until the mine was actually BUILT, so my dad's job was to sell promises that everything was going to go smoothly. Meanwhile, the owner of the whole operation was getting sued for taking everyone's contract money and basically sitting on it. Yet another lesson about the corruption that corporate entities welcome and how much, and usually is, put up for gamble regarding honest people and families on the line who are deceived. My father had to pick up some odd jobs in order to keep everything afloat and it was a rather dark time in the dynasty. This reevaluation of life causes people to turn to Faith and to God, for we are ignorant people. He went from poking fun towards the priest to referring to bible verses in conversation. My sister and I rejected this and saw religion as weakness, much like how his side of the family was raised. Or more so, a private worship, as if you didn't want anyone to catch you praying or reading the bible in fear of appearing weak and foolish. I knew that God and Faith cannot be forced onto me, and my father understood this in time...

The Beacon

Flashing forward about 2 years… I'm at the Beacon (Crow's parent's house aka the Beacon) which holds a lot of memories; from shirtless acid trips to one of us attempting to slide down the rail of the winding staircase (while intoxicated) with the result of making it about two inches down the rail before the pants caught traction on the sticky wood and falling about 20 feet straight onto his face on a hard wooden floor. Good times…

As we bake in the scorching Florida sun, I receive a call from a friend in Michigan, which doesn't usually happen out of the blue. The call was from a close friend named Paul. "Paul my boy, what's cookin'?", I say jovially. The reason I knew something was up because I didn't even receive a courtesy laugh. Paul let out a slow reply, "Hey man, I wanted to call you because Joe is currently in the ER on Life Support, he tried to kill himself". Long pause.

This was the first time since my parent's divorce where I got that feeling deep in my stomach, the feeling where a panic and paranoia unlike any other begins to burn in the pit of the soul. How do I process this? Should I cry? I feel like there should be tears, but none came. I walked away from my friends without saying a word and looked out over the palm trees that provided a border between the Beacon and the house next door. I then sort of melted onto the floor as the energy gave out in my legs. "What happened?" was all I was able to ask, "I walked in on him after he tried to hang himself, he was unconscious already", Paul replied. I was searching frantically in my head for the right words and how things arrived at that point. "I had no idea he felt this way… I wish I could've helped him or at least understand what he is going through" I responded slowly with an undertone of desperate confusion. Paul then provided his perspective, "He was dropping a lot of acid and getting really deep into his head, I don't think any of us really could have done anything man, we tried the best we could." Paul was trying to be as reassuring as he could muster out. I could tell he was still processing all of it still as much as I was, since Joe wasn't the type of person to do this… But who really is?

"Thank you for letting me know, you're a good friend and please keep me updated" I didn't want to bathe in grief as he wasn't gone yet, but by the sound of things, there wasn't much left that could be done. Paul replied, "I definitely will, love you brother." Paul concluded. End call.

The rest of the day consisted of me being in this sort of dissociative daze, I explained everything to my friends that had just witnessed the call with the most silence I have ever witnessed out of them. None of them have had a similar experience, so they didn't really know what to say and I didn't blame them. I went home rather early to my Dad's place at the time; a small house in the 'more-affordable' side of town, an interesting and largely misunderstood mixture of people. I sat for a while and thought about how a soul like Joe's can be distorted in such a way for him to actually do it. I mean, many of us have contemplated ending our lives due to the environment around us and the eternal emptiness that can accompany not being able to truly express oneself to those around you, the potential peace and serenity in giving up. But this is a very sad distortion that my good friend Joe was able to teach me about that day. In these moments I see how life is meant to be cherished and enjoyed, and the low depths that our hearts and minds can be brought to when one is not mentally prepared for intense emotions that are awakened using psychedelics and/or environmental stress in general that seems to build up over time.

My best friend died that day.

June 1st, 2015:

Freshly graduated high school, ready to break through the shackles...

It's interesting, the feeling in the air among graduating kids who have no idea what they want in life, just happy to be done with this BS institution and pumped full of anxious hormonal energy.

It is interesting how it becomes hard to look back on that time, no matter how miserable, without a hint of nostalgia for those four (more or less) years, mixed with the feeling of wanting to run as far away as possible without looking back. A collective youth spending a length of time together in a controlled environment, confused, scared and in the need of proper mentorship. After this nostalgia quickly evaporated, I was ready to go wild: more freedom, more opportunity for disaster, a whole flood of impulses. Looking in hindsight, I can see how much a friend group influences the members within and affects the decision making as a group. I was able to mold to many different crowds, shapeshift in order to fit in and not raise too many questions, for I had no real identity, a shadow. Life in those days had become a game of manipulation and mask-wearing. It could be greatly due to the neuroses of the area; materialistic, appearance based, money motivated. But the area is only as good as the people within, and many of these people are lost, including me. I grew to enjoy being the Chameleon, the Mockingbird, the Entertainer, anything but the person I wanted to become.

The Rave/EDM (electronic dance music) scene was popping off at the time and what better way to kick off graduating high school than with an end-of-year rave at Club Babble, the cheapest yet most popular club in our area? Not much!

Like many young adults on the rise and on the hunt, we were experimenting with drugs. Since the passing of my best friend Joe, I always kept a cautious eye on this in my subconscious. However, that night, against my better judgement, I chose to try Ecstasy. Fast-forwarding a few hours into the night… We were at the club: dark, damp, always smelling of cigarettes and dirty intentions. We were getting our groove on with the Techni-colored lasers and flashing lights entranced the crowd and then, BOOM, I started to lose consciousness. My frame of vision dilated like a pupil until all was black, as if I fell asleep while still awake. All the surrounding color and form in my peripheral vision shrunk into a tiny, nonexistent space.

This was the first time in my life where I was doing and saying things, but nobody was home, I would come back into the light about once every 20 minutes, almost like an internal alarm clock going off, in order to make sure that I didn't hurt anyone or do something excessively stupid. Throughout the night I am mumbling random sentences to my friends, grabbing random people that I thought looked familiar… It seemed funny at the time, but it was terrifying how one can lose themselves completely to a chemical vortex, yet how freely and openly they are used in society. Something doesn't feel right about that. However, in the fog of the night, there was this one moment of clarity: when my eyes first interlocked with hers. I had to make that dramatic because it was much like one of those Fairy Tale stories that you didn't think really happen

As if stolen directly from the Goddess realm and by some strange anomaly has wandered into my field of vision, we had a mutual friend who introduced us.

Her hair was dirty blonde like mine, with these beautiful round blue eyes and one of those noses that split down the middle and slightly butterflied along the tip, giving a distinct appearance of elegance and aesthetic, kind of like a cat or fox. She had freckles on her face, but just the right amount to evade the eye at a quick glance. Her body was slender, but the curves were evident and proportional to her body in a lovely way… I was awestruck, it was almost as if my dream woman, Dreya, was copied from my brain and pasted there right in front of me, I figured the ecstasy was playing a role as well...

I probably looked like a lost little boy as I was staring at her, processing all of it. We all grouped together on the upper level of the club in order to enjoy the rest of the night as a group. In order to catch her attention without directly showing my interest, I made a quick decision and began performing this strange 'running-in-place' dance move as if I was running on an imaginary treadmill. My shirt was off, and I was glistening with sweat, but I didn't care, I loved everybody.

Somehow the tactic worked, as I sat down after my improvisation, she leaned over with this ear-to-ear grin, which sort of reminded me of Olivia Newton-John from the classic movie *Grease*, and she screamed into my ear, "That was hilarious!" Her voice was shrill and high pitched but had a sweetness to it. "Why, thank you", I replied in a cheeky, flirtatious voice. "I'm Calysta" she responded after tapping her cigarette close to the ground, watching the accumulated ash plop onto the musty black carpet. I replied a few seconds later without breaking my glance, "I'm Zeal."

We went through the initial motions and didn't say much to each other after that because the club was loud, as it should be. "She can't be from here..." I thought to myself. She has the indifference and thick skin of a northerner but the spark and sass of a California girl. My mind was racing all over but I could only enjoy the music. That night I felt something that I have never felt before. We exchanged information with the distant assurance that we will see each other in the future. I secretly dreaded the thought of possibly not being able to see her again, as we do with random beauties that come and go

within our lives.

A Brief Love Story

Since that fateful day, Caly and I inevitably started spending time together more frequently and getting to know each other. Within a few months, we were inseparable. I had never met someone so free and yet, so trapped and secretly scared. So beautiful yet coming from such ugliness and betrayal. One night when we were laying together on my dad's couch, she smelled like cigarettes, a hard smell to get used to but it developed a romantic edge to it as it blended in with her personality and beauty. She told me about how her mother was rarely around, and she had a drug problem, leaving her oblivious father to fulfill both roles of mommy and daddy. I felt compassion towards her, and I wanted to care for her and devote all of my time and energy to loving her. Calysta was my goddess, a goddess that I had no idea how to worship.

Something notable about the transition between high school and college is that the wave of transitional energy affects everyone differently. With that being mentioned, Caly and I were quickly developing traits of an immature married couple; tension/jealousy arising if one chooses to spend time with friends, constant paranoia and suspicions of adultery, which is a clear sign of a lack of trust and unaddressed childhood issues. All of this, coupled with a lack of communication, caused a lot of growing resentment towards one another, which was completely overwhelming for me. Another note, or more of a friendly warning, is to be cautious of the Gemini woman. Those who have experienced will understand and, in time, the reference will reveal itself to the seeker of True Love who has encountered deception… I digress.

'My son, be attentive to my wisdom; incline your ear to my understanding, that you may keep discretion, and your lips may guard knowledge. For the lips of the strange woman drip honey, and her speech is smoother than oil, but in the end, she is bitter as wormwood, sharp as a two edged sword. Her feet go down to death; her steps follow the path to Hell; she does not ponder the path of life; her ways wander, as she does not know it.' - Proverbs 5:1-6

Choice of friends and social environment had played an annoyingly large but necessary role in my relationship with Calysta, for jealousy and tension also arises among friends and family. Not everyone is out to get you, but people do tend to project their insecurities and depravities on those who they think have what they don't.

Taking all of this in and keeping it mostly in my head, dismissing all of my thoughts as over-sensitive paranoia, the natural tendency was to bury these observations and hope they die.

Huge mistake. I wrote a poem:

The Pendulum

As it swings, As it goes

There is no stopping the singing crows

The dagger that drives, with thine own hand the culprit

No one knows

With Father Time, I sit by the fire

Watching the embers dance

He tells me of a lost history

A soft, loving choir

A divinity left to Free-Will and Chance

Sweet blossom, please bloom

For I crave your Spring

The Darkness in my soul

Many disruptive thought-demons does it bring

My Dear, My Love

Beat onto my drum

As we sway on this eternal dance

Like the Pendulum

In hindsight, I realize that a course-changing wrong turn that I made was shutting down, something I had perfected as a boy. To dissociate eliminates emotion and attachment to the given situation, but ultimately, it is a defense mechanism and a way of escaping. Defense mechanisms aren't necessarily bad, but when they become the norm, we form the anxiety and pressure of a much-needed change. If we feel that we need to numb ourselves in order to get through life, to keep a cycle going that rarely ever leads one 'above the surface', then why do we truly live? I begin to grow passive and cold, a lot like my father became when my parents divorced earlier in my life. It is interesting how we replay these tracks unconsciously.

Flash forwards a year…

Caly and I have spent nearly every day together and I have lost touch with many of my friends and myself, but I could care less about that, I'm in love.

We held each other tight for hours, as if we were going to forget each other at any moment. It was exhilarating, my blood had never run that hot to the mere touch of a woman, but it did with her. We were both so different from each other, yet it was as if we were together in past lifetimes, so that every layer of misunderstanding was trumped by our ancient lover's tale. I didn't get this feeling whilst smoking pot with my friends. Granted, Caly and I indulged in the flower, but it seems to be a more spiritual experience with someone you love. Yet, twice as maddening.

She allowed me to see dimensions to her that lived and hid beyond the facade of her beautiful smile… Pure and unconditional. I also revealed dimensions of myself that I didn't even know existed, they didn't need to exist before her. Calysta is teaching me something about life that has caused me many sleepless nights and long walks on the beach. If I can find this treasure through raw emotion and coincidence with someone so different and so much more reckless than I, what does that mean for all of us? This realization was bigger than me and I began to silently and internally panic. Why would I panic? People would kill to feel something like this, right?

It was exactly that. Why are we so desperate to get lost into other people? Why would someone feel the need to rob someone of their love for someone else? Is there that little love inside of us to go around?

As my thoughts and questions became louder and seemingly more urgent, I felt that Calysta was beginning to fade away, or maybe it was I who was fading away from the entire situation.

She liked to drink... Frequently. She liked to party…

Frequently. She liked to have sex… Frequently. This started to

become (all humor aside) demanding and exhausting. I would

like to make it clear that I'm not just some robot that doesn't

enjoy sexual intercourse, but the whole affair started to become

excessive and almost forced, with the Love fading away with

my willpower...

It is safe to say that we have become so overtly sexualized as a

society that kids can't wait to ultimately let the tides of

immorality take them for a ride.

I began to feel like a square and an old man for starting to crave

values and morals, but I didn't have the strength or

commitment. I felt like a Steppenwolf, beautifully and painfully

coined by Hermann Hesse, a wolf of the steps, a lone wolf

constantly pacing up and down the staircase and not knowing

where to go.

Then started the dawn of infidelity. Since this was my first real

love experience, I didn't know what to do regarding attraction

towards other women and developing moral standards of my

own. This spans back to observing the broken marriage that

served as my main example, that of my parents. I always had the underlying suspicion that she was never faithful, and once I found some revealing texts on her phone while she was sleeping in my bed, I slipped. We were around 19-20 years old at the time. Every minute of cheating on my beloved felt forced and terrible, I then knew what all the fuss was about and why one of the Commandments is 'Thou shalt not commit adultery', for it is a vile act that corrupts the soul.

Consequently, there was a night soon where I was waiting for Caly to come home from a drunken night at the beach with her so-called friends. She wasn't responding to me, so I texted one of the friends who was with her. "She was dropped off a little while ago by David',' was the reply, which was enough for me to drive to her place (her dad wasn't home, conveniently) since I was unaware of this mystery character. I opened the door (it wasn't locked) and I walked upstairs, cautiously but with wrath and purpose. The small staircase unfolded into their small living room furnished with an old brown velvet couch, coffee table, and T.V.

That burning feeling when you know that something you fear is right around the corner. It was dark in the room, but not dark enough. On the couch I observed a man with his shirt off with Calysta next to him with a sweatshirt on… sound asleep.

I walked up to them with no words and the glowing eyes of a cat slowly and cautiously inching towards its prey. I looked at them for a few seconds, my pupils must have been huge, taking in every possible shred of evidence that I could present to the jury of betrayal. The mystery man was awake since I had reached the top of the stairs, still groggy but knowing perfectly well that he was in the wrong place at the wrong time, or maybe I was...

He saw me staring at him, then her, then back at him. I reached over him and shook Calysta's shoulder in order to wake her up, I wanted her to be awake. She grumbled and mumbled with her eyes still closed. As soon as I heard a noise come out of the mystery man's mouth and was reminded, he was there, I started uncontrollably punching; hammers, jabs, hooks to the side of his skull... I covered every square inch of his face. His only immediate defense was sticking his arms straight out in desperation, pushing my face to the side while I continued to deliver my heavy mechanical blows until all I heard was a gurgling sound and his arms dropped. I never knew how hard the human face is.

I left the house and felt nothing but blood. Boiling blood in my eyes, hands, and fingertips. I looked down at my right hand and saw the pinky knuckle was compressed down towards the middle of my hand. I didn't feel a thing. It was the first time I

ever hit anyone, first time I completely lost control of my
emotions... and Calysta was sleeping soundly...

That night is also the first that I have broken down emotionally
in front of my sister, who never really went out (cancer sun
sign= homebody), and saw me walking into my dad's house;
head drooped down with my right arm hanging limp, the pain
started to kick in about now. I just sat on her bed next to her
and started sobbing, "What happened?!" my kind, reserved
sister asked. "She was with someone else" was all I could
squeeze out. Lexi didn't say much but she gave me a little hug
and did the best she could, and I appreciated her endlessly for
that. My dad was snoozed-out drunk on the couch and there
was a smaller, personalized dark cloud hanging over my head. I
didn't expect them to fully understand, but they were the only
people that were anywhere close to understanding me.

(03/26/16)- *I know, you missed me. I regretfully admit that I
have been slacking on documenting my rather cloudy life. An
explanation for my absence can consist of school, work, and
recently getting my heart torn out of my chest and dumped on.
Calysta, the love of my life, has taken it upon herself to end our
reign of passion and love. It's honestly for the better and I
deserve way more than what she has taken away from me. But*

the depressing and crippling fact of the matter is... I don't want

better or more, just her. I don't know why, and I don't know

how, but I have been enchanted and mesmerized by this

succubus. Love is the most powerful and dangerous force on

this Earth if we don't wield it properly. Throughout our 8-

month inseparable attachment, I was able to see the light and

divine beauty that had become broken and dark, by forces that

she seems to still be unaware of. I get this feeling that she and I

both know and still feel... maybe that goes away with time. I

often think about her and wonder if she thinks about me. It's an

exhausting spiritual and emotional dance, this is. Both dancers

don't have to be equal in skill, but both have to willingly

synchronize in order to accomplish something surreal and

beautiful.

I have every reason to delete her from my worry list, but there's

something, a little dust bunny that constantly blows around the

desert of my mind, aimlessly, running into different obstacles in

said desert. For some reason I cannot trap that dust bunny. It

stays there, lingers, waiting for the optimal time to irritate my

mind's eye. I have so much love to provide, so much intimacy I

want to share... But with who? Caly? HA! Maybe in another

lifetime.

A Fallen Angel

It is interesting how a first love can leave a scar… a memory of something that didn't end how it felt like it was 'supposed to'. We both discovered that we were on separate wavelengths, living in two different worlds under the same roof, two different pages in the same book. I had exhausted my reserves of energy with the petty and the fake, and she began to realize we were both holding onto a fantasy. A departure from a first love without proper closure can cause a paranoia and insecurity that bleeds into everyday relationships and interactions if we don't take the proper measures to address these residues. This can cause the self-induced victim (me) to go through a rather rude awakening process. I began to examine thoroughly what truly matters in life and how we can get swept up if we're not aware. However, the beauty and intelligence of the universe allows us to make these mistakes and learn from them organically, or not, the choice is ultimately ours.

As I explore my Mind and Soul, it begins to become more evident that we, as humans, are vessels; containers and transmitters of energies and the invisible forces at work around us. We are antennae for the energies that swim all around us and through us. I was too eager to lose myself to the first

entrancing pair of glossy blue eyes that understood me and

smiled at me with the right smile. How prevalent the insecurity

is within our western society; supermodels on every TV

commercial, yet a McDougal's fast-food chain on every street

corner, the ability to suck fat out of a body and stitch it right

back up if one has the money, as well as prostitution and

pornography running rampant through the streets, allowing

little authentic communication and relationship. It just doesn't

feel right, does it? This subtle change that seems to be coming

from a distance...

"To his cabinet; he dreamt of being on a singular and

indescribable vessel that was moving with great rapidity

toward a dark and indefinite shore" - Abraham Lincoln's

recollection of a frequent dream.

Men and women are confused and lost… the children watch

with innocent helplessness, but I hear their calls. I haven't lost

my way completely, although the path has been shrouded in

darkness and shadows. I still see the Light. Money and Power

have become our Gods, security and te(lie)vision our

shepherds. The song is Orwellian with an overtone of Huxley,

observing in the background silently and intently are Hesse and

Jung. I sit in a tent in the wooded pine, I see a black beetle on

the vine, soft hum of the swamp. I have committed material

treason of the highest degree, for I have abandoned my job and my fees, to live among the trees and the breeze where love is an abundant wellspring. I sit and smile softly; all I need is this moment… but I begin to worry about what comes after. My eyes shoot open as they proceed to dart from side to side; alert… anxious… paranoid… What is this? This disgusting feeling... Where am I?

I feel so distant from home, so far away from my heart and who I was a few long years ago. I need to remain faithful, through this storm we shall pass. My body begins to feel heavier, I never realized there was weight to it until now. Father, Mother, what did I do wrong?

Nothing my child, your journey has just begun.

What are angels? The word itself seems to be curiously similar to 'angles', as in different angles or expressions of light perhaps? An example from the Bible, Hebrews 1:14: 'Are not all angels ministering spirits sent to serve those who will inherit salvation?' and Hebrews 13:2: 'Do not forget to show hospitality to strangers, for by so doing, some people have shown hospitality to angels without knowing it.' These verses are interesting to me because it seems that we crave the Hollywood excitement in our daily lives, yet God is more subtle and loving, for we can stumble across guardian angels without even realizing. It could even be your cat or dog.

Is it crazy to think that humans themselves could be a wave or offspring of fallen angels? Without descending onto the Earth through birth and forgetting who we are, experiencing the sufferings and the joys that allow us to come back to Source, God, the Infinite Creator through Free Will, how would it be a truly fair test? We develop these bonds with the Earth when we are born and begin to have an energetic and spiritual impact upon Her, for the Earth is alive and a receptive feminine organism, the Sun being masculine, and all of us being the light cells operating upon the Mother through the Will of the Infinite Source, God, which works individually through each of us. Our decisions and emotions ripple through the outer and inner skies and we have the choice to transcend and transmute our lower desires and the illusion trap of materialism, which, in turn, allows us to experience the realm of Heaven from which we came and shall return. On the other hand, we also have the choice to remain slaves to ourselves and live in Hell (the unbalanced and distorted Mind and Heart). I'm not saying I'm all peaches and gravy, but the groundwork is laid out for us all and we were given the divine right to freely choose how we would like to serve, whether that be unconsciously or with awareness. For you, for me, for raising the vibration of the Human Race and rid the corruption that has been running wild and confidently through the fields. You and I are related, and I hope to meet you one day, whether in this life or the next. If you are reading this, you hold a piece of my soul.

We may have fallen but we shall rise again, as was always intended.

(Rubik's Puzzle)- Confusion, clouded thoughts leading to regretful decisions. It's a jigsaw puzzle but all the pieces shift and change at your own hand, like a Rubik's cube. People like to simplify life by comparing it to one sole action or thing, whereas it is more of a mixture of things working in harmony with one's daily life. Some may call it God's plan, some may call it karma, and others think everything is within their control. I seem to be stuck somewhere in the middle; I feel like many are as well. There is nothing that satisfies me more than the Truth, no matter how unappealing or hurtful it may be. What would we do without this mysterious guiding force? I'm so confused... 19 years old, not sure what I really want to do with my life, not knowing what to believe and what to avoid. My anthropology teacher last year told me that God and religion are used merely as a way of coping with anxieties and stresses of everyday life. But my dad went from never going to church and bashing religion to reading the bible every day and turning to Jesus as his Lord and Savior, which feels right in a way. I'm so confused... I wish it could all come clear as day, but what's the fun in that?

__August 30th, 2017:__ I'm becoming increasingly more unstable which scares me. I went to Calysta's when I got off of work and I'm falling in love with her again. Everything about her makes my heart warm and kissing her makes me forget about anything bad in this world. She loves someone else now. I feel like I have many regrets in my short life and I just want to be sure of something for once. I want to know what I truly want without following lust like I have so many times in the past. I want clarity. After Calysta's I went home, and I saw that I was dropped from my classes because I didn't pay for them by the deadline and I had a little mental break-down. My mom, bless her heart, tried making things better but I was in the abyss of my mind, almost in a catatonic and dissociated state. It's getting worse and I need to stabilize myself one way or another before I officially go crazy (this is one of the entries that inspired Zeal to go vegetarian, since red meat and animal meat in general is known to cause inflammation in the body and brain, which can lead to brain fog and confusion as well as other manifestations). Love is the most powerful form of magic.

Apocalypse (Lifting of the Veil) ...

Feeling an indescribable frustration and anger… feeling crushed by an invisible force, so subtle.

What's going on? I felt like there was some sort of circuit wiring that has been reattached after 20 years of atrophy and dust-gathering, almost as if I didn't deserve this new-found clarity and perception, to sense other people's emotions and thoughts as if they were my own… This was like an intrusion that I couldn't understand, let alone control. Like a cocktail of memories, thoughts, flashes from my past that started flooding my view like a swirling sea of light, I had to sit down. All I could do was wait for this mental lightning storm to pass, like I was a damned schizoid. It kind of makes sense now… are crazy people *really* crazy? What is crazy, truly? Do we just fear and dismiss what we don't have the capability and 'time' to understand? There have been times where I thought I knew everything I needed to, but as time goes on and I am allowed to see and feel more through my developing love for God within me and connecting to the God within everyone else, the more I realize I don't know squat.

August 19th, 2017: The air feels strange, like I'm living in a haze. I see people, but I'm not sure what I see. Calysta asked me to come over at around 1:30am and I went. I missed her. It has been too long since I've been able to feel her in my arms and see her beautiful smile that plucks me out from whatever depression I seem to put myself into at the time. I love when she comes to realize that I am the key to her locked heart. She was drunk when I saw her, I could smell it on her. She drank some wine with her friend Olivia because she recently found out that she was pregnant and the baby belongs to a guy that cheated on her, funny how that works. Caly told me that she read a letter I wrote to her two years prior when we first started dating. She loves the way I write to her. We caught up, we kissed, felt each other like we used to. I started to kiss her neck and moved down towards her breasts. It was a good feeling, her lips on mine, her warm, pale skin underneath my fingertips. I'm more confused now than I was before. I have this weird paranoia that she is of reptilian descent and is feeding off my energy. My captivation towards her is just a mystery to me so I look for metaphysical ways to justify it. I'm a mess.

The Haze (2018)-

I wake up in a world of fire

Flames of lust and greed surmount love and compassion

Worrying how we're going to get the next best car or large mansion

I am here in a haze, a cloudy blissful gaze

Where the secrets hide in a matter of ways

The curtain is closing, the Grand Master composing

an ignorant orchestra, of which no one cares to listen

Keep your eye on the Sun's magnificent rays

For we are all living in a haze.

(Date unmarked, drawing of Gothic all-seeing eye in the title space)- *Lately I've been growing more and more restless. Sometimes I think of dying in my sleep so that I can live in a world of my own creation. No pain, no hope, no BS. We always want what we can't have and what ends up being toxic to us, yet we do it anyway. I don't know where I'm going. I am a lost soul in an infinite river of lost souls. Everywhere I go I see fakeness, deceit, insecurity covered with a light mask. I want to be a source of light, I need faith, a Higher Power. I want to live in a world that I enjoy without feeling the need to depend on substances outside of myself. I am miserable without weed; I am miserable without love. I make reckless decisions despite all of the walls I've run into and lessons I've been taught. I seem to be a fool in a fool's paradise. My soul feels broken, along with my heart. Evil is winning, the light and color are fading from my vision, enveloped in an unforgiving yet brutally humbling* *darkness. Why did I get a kitten? I need to cleanse my body as well as my soul. I want to feel the divine light wash every inch of my being and feel the rejuvenation of rebirth.*

April 2nd- *As the days go by, things just get weirder and weirder. I feel the tides shifting, my mind leaving my physical body as well as this physical realm. There is so much to be learned and understood in this world of boredom and over-informing on the same mindless subjects. We are constantly looking for stimulus, something to constantly distract or worry about, it's exhausting. My current mission is to gain peace of mind, since my head feels like a can of worms that was blown open with a shotgun. My other goal is to stay out of jail. My probation is almost over yet I can't stop smoking to save my life. I'm just weak minded right now and bitter. I have a scratch behind my ear which makes me think I was microchipped in my sleep, but that's probably the paranoia talking. My dissociation has gotten worse too, granted, it could be from the caffeine consumption causing me to feel 'out-of-body' and aids in my lack of concentration.*

Anima- *I sit staring forward for an hour or two*

Thoughts like static flicker their way to you

Flashing lights, shill shriek, there is blood on my hands

Silver-streaked runner

Skipping in the sands

As color returns, revealing the scrapes and burns

I see the tower with the window while the small hand turns

My anima, the one I created

She comes when I want her

Hides when I need her

For she is me

And I am She

The Dragonfly

There is a decision that each of us are faced with at a certain point; we can either conform a.k.a. 'sell-out' and let this financial system that we live in guide us into mindlessness and insanity, or we can claim ourselves from ourselves and strive to live in mental and spiritual liberty. This decision is something I have been trying to wrap my head around. Do I keep thinking all day and night about it? Do I put my head down, shut up, and keep working for a system I don't believe in until I die? The latter scares the gravy off my grits and the fact that this thinking already places me against the grain may be even more frightening. I realize that I could be on my own on this one... but this is a different sense of loneliness, a penetrating, deep-boned loneliness that not even the wolves could satisfy with a desperate howl at the moon. Do others have these thoughts? I need some insight, but from where? From whom?

I have tried talking to my parents, but when they're struggling to keep afloat as well, one begins to stop asking. Not to sound bitter and that I don't appreciate the effort, they try the best they can, given the circumstances. I have tried therapy, which is interesting, and I was able to have educated conversations regarding the questions I had about the field of Psychology, such as dream analysis, which I was heavily into and was also reading *The Interpretation of Dreams* by Sigmund Freud (I am more of a Carl Jung pupil but this book seems to be a gateway to dream analysis for many) at the time. I quickly found out that I wasn't schizophrenic, mostly a wound up and unbalanced ball of energy with a clinical case of disillusionment. I am beginning to realize that fear has been slowly closing in on me.

Then came my first run-in with the law, learning first-hand how one can get arrested through possession of a smokable plant.

Being in the county jail for approximately 22 hours allowed me to obtain a brief glimpse of the 'belly of the beast', if you will. Around 30 floors of misled, misunderstood, and corrupted souls that have been left to be forgotten and wither away within colorless walls. Harboring hatred and resentment for everyone and everything, especially themselves. An interesting factor, which I was un-equipped for, was having to memorize phone numbers. They do not provide Yellow Pages (phone book) in the slammer, meaning that one would have to remember the phone number of their lifeline to the outside world in order to have any hope of getting bailed out, or else join the rest of the forgotten. The only number that I had memorized was my father's, who was currently in Costa Rica on his honeymoon with his second wife (lovely woman).

First call… No answer.

Starting to feel the hope evaporate from my cold body. Another inconvenient aspect of the jail system is that instead of the call going through normally, the receiver has to agree to pay for the call per-minute, causing more frustration and angst for the parties involved. It seems like they really want you to stick around.

Second call… Click! "Hello?" I heard my dad's husky voice.

"Hey dad, I'm so sorry to bother you on your honeymoon… I know the timing is perfect. But can you please call or text mom and tell her that I'm in jail? I forgot her number and I would

really like to get out of here". I let out the best sarcastic chuckle

that I could, which sounded more like a wheeze. I tried to

squeeze everything into one quick sentence without leaving

room for potential wrath and ridicule.

"I'll get in touch with her right away, are you okay?", was my

dad's heroic reply, if you give him the cold hard facts, he'll

pick what you're laying down and cut to the chase when

necessary. I replied as reassuring as I could, "Yeah, I'm alright,

I was just in the wrong place at the wrong time. I don't want to

keep you but thank you for picking up and I love you." I

concluded. That was rough, trying not to let out some tears of

realization in front of 'the boys' (fellow jail mates). I ended up

making some unexpected friends (not what you think) who

were really decent people that got caught up in some indecent

lifestyles and seem to get severely punished with little hope of

reconciliation. A lot of folks seemed to be forced into coming

to God within themselves, because in that place there is

nowhere else you can go but within, no matter how pissed off

you are.

I was brought down to the in-house courtroom where they hold

mini hearings/sentences. Sitting atop a little wooden throne was the judge of lost souls wearing his black robes of death, this particular one had gray hair and glasses and looked sort of like what comes to mind when you think of a 5th grade Christian math teacher. I have always found it fascinating… a man or woman who goes to law school has the actual right to make decisions regarding the fate of someone's life. Not to mention, many of these judges and law-enforcers are scoundrels themselves, which adds to the painful humor and irony.

There were people that were sentenced and then proceeded to threaten to kill themselves in order to be deemed 'psychologically unstable' in hopes of being sent to the psych ward. This somewhat ensures safety from the pit bulls on the main floor and brings forth the opportunity to get sedated with drugs, depending on how good of an actor they are, or perhaps how irritating they can be to the guards. The interesting and sad part about these people threatening to hurt themselves was that the guards and officers working in the jail encourage these inmates to hurt themselves, antagonizing them to the point of truly questioning their sanity. This was like something out of a goddamned movie; here I am, a little blonde, Caucasian boy in here for marijuana… I could almost laugh.

My bail was set at $600.00; the judge saw that I was a chicken in a den of wolves and probably felt a little chink in his armor.

I was returned to my cell and woke up the next morning expecting it all to have been a dream. No matter how hard I tried to change my perception and de-materialize out of that joint like a ghost, it didn't work. I missed Calysta, I missed sunlight. I had only been in here a night and It felt like a year.

One of my friends, Chase, was my saviour of the situation and bailed me out, for whom I hold a great respect and gratitude towards for life.

I was then placed on two years of probation for this lunacy, a babe in the woods of Law and Order. So much rage and frustration filled my days and nights; having to sell my car in order to pay for the money-hungry attorneys, having my mother drive me to court so that I can perform this music-less dance with the court, pitiful. I see how, in hindsight, I was able to learn about the corruption within the legal/court system and come out with minimal damage and being able to tell the tale. However, at the time my life was in a dark age. Never had I felt so lost, so angry, so utterly hopeless. In these moments, nothing anyone said to me could console the gloomy darkness that was blocking my soul. These pivotal moments are those that change a person's life, either towards a path of feeding the lower emotions and desires and self-destruction, or the path of learning, loving, and exaltation through connection with one's own Soul. The latter sounds exhausting, but it seems to be the most effective way I will survive.

This time period feels like being underwater, yet you never

drown. Just the constant anxiety of not being able to breathe

fresh air.

The Old Wizard

He sits in his cell

Mad genius behind the lids

All in Sight and Mind

Yet, nothing is his.

No crime committed, people filled the cracks

A scapegoat for evil

A lamb for the racks

No hope, it seems

Can't see the sunbeams

All within Sight and Mind

Yet, nothing is his.

No wrong, no right

Short day, long night

The Old Wizard never has to fight

With a heart of Gold, he quickly grows old

He was told and the rest was sold

Nothing is as it seems.

So, you must look within the sunbeams of Love and Truth

Placed on the forehead

He lays quietly in his small bed, seeing the life he has grown

through

The life he has left behind.

This sobering epiphany applied to more than just being on probation, this reflects the macrocosm (the big picture) within the microcosm (personal life and daily situations), for everyone has their own fears and setbacks that we often ignore or place on the back burner until a house-fire eventually starts. We learn to take in minimal life-oxygen and get used to the drowning feeling, we forget what fresh air is like and how vital it truly is. I had to go back to the beginning, the crumbs that I have swept under the rug that are now beginning to attract ants. I had to salvage the disregarded parts of my story and show them love

and attention so that I can repair and grow into what I am
meant to be, a vessel of Love, of Truth.

Along the distant shore appeared some lost hope to the whole
scenario. Since I was digging myself a grave of guilt and
shame, I put down the shovel and called an end to the pity
party. What is experience without learning and struggle? What
is a successful invention without trial and error? We tend to
grow so fearful of a bumpy road that we are too fearful to
embark on the journey at all, why is this? A lot of great
questions! Through extensive thought and reflection on the
subject, it seems that this whole fear complex is not accidental.
We are taught and indoctrinated through our corrupted
education system to become robotic, neurotic workers who
operate according to the Holy algorithm of 'Efficiency', which
has no room for pesky human error or creativity. Through
generations of killing creativity and the soul in order to become
the 'best' and the most 'politically correct', which parents learn
to encourage and eventually lock themselves into competition
over along with fellow parents. Comparing whose child is the
best at conforming. The rest seemed to naturally weave itself
out into what we have today,

What do you think? This line of questioning can even take one
back to the perceived beginning, when our soul first incarnated
in this realm. On this current 3-dimensional Earth plane, it
seems that if we are not aware and integrated, as we are

targeted at the earliest age. We have to deal with painful physical and emotional experiences in order to inspire change in our self-destructive and ignorant lives. On the other hand, there are those who seem to be 'asleep' yet breeze through life with little resistance and minimal effort. I believe the explanation for this dynamic is that it cannot really be explained universally, only felt/processed on an individual level. A key is to practice 'big picture' thinking and view our existence as an energetic dance of the different soul expressions of God, the one Infinite Love. In between moments of despair and hopelessness, there are intense glimmers of Truth; undeniable, unfiltered truth that justice cannot be ode to through human words, yet, we have all had these experiences in one way or another that cannot be ignored.

It feels like putting together pieces of a puzzle that are not bound by time or by density but are constantly being shifted and worked on behind the scenes with unconditional love, ever-changing and growing according to our Free will. These moments have started to pop up way too often to keep shoved down, naturally making this study, wherever it may lead me, a part of my mission.

March 15th- *It's been about two full days now since I have been in this haze. For some reason I get into this trance-like, dissociated state and my mind overpowers my body when trying to stop smoking weed. I have a month left of probation, but my*

P.O. (probation officer) was switched a few weeks before which threw my whole case back a couple of months. Hey, don't worry, it's just my life! Life is testing me, per-usual, as well as my family. I swear we are cursed sometimes because my mom always has bad luck, or maybe just makes poor decisions, but she's always strong enough to endure it. Talk about that ancient divine strength of the Latina woman. There is a dark energy in the world, and it feels like it is only going to get thicker. There are shockingly accurate bible prophecies that have clearly come true, eliminating the previous skepticism that I had towards the scriptures. We are about to enter a dark age of panic and chaos that none of us will be able to handle unless we go within and listen...

What is the point? Is all of this for nothing? I guess that's one of the big questions. Often, during probation, I would go out to a nature trail located within a nearby Japanese-style garden and establish a relationship with the beautiful healing powers of nature. I had been losing myself in all sorts of information and 'rabbit-holes' in order to 'keep my mind occupied' which is a common excuse for avoiding addressing my internal issues and is easy to perpetuate in the Age of Technology and instant information and distraction. I was getting into faeries and elemental beings, as well as other esoteric topics that would help elevate me from my funk, and how there are 'gateways' in undisturbed nature settings that connect with these hidden realms if one is pure of Heart and Will. I had noticed a lot of dragonflies zipping around the sky, always hovering in little clumps above where I was walking or standing, almost as if they were following me, observing my actions. I'm not sure if I was just paranoid, but since I am interested in the subject of faeries, I consciously search for signs. This train of thought then took the next stop at realizing that our degrees of consciousness affect our direct moods and perceptions, so, what if faeries and elementals are always around, we just aren't at the proper frequency and/or vibration to see them or connect with them? What if they're not hiding, we are just too ignorant and see what we want to see? The flurry of thought encouraged me to sit down on the trail and listen, not for anything specific, just for the thoughts to pass peacefully and bring forth anything relevant or useful, or not. Fantastically enough, a dragonfly hovered over me and proceeded to perch on a small weed popping out of the Earth.

Dragonflies have always creeped me out, do they bite? What do they see? But in this moment, we felt like old friends, sort of funny. I just stared at this insect, observing it like they had observed me overhead. Upon closer inspection of the little dragon, I noticed a rainbow-colored shimmer emanating from the translucent wings of the dragonfly. Am I delusional from the heat? I leaned in for a closer look, which the Dragonfly permitted, and noticed that the wings themselves reflected light, depending on the angle that you looked at them, into a beautiful rainbow shimmer. They seemed like built-in solar panels that the dragonfly charges up on its little grass perch. This probably allowed the insect to consume less physical material and operate more on light energy, like a hybrid car. I was losing myself in the beautiful cosmic design of these wings, it started to dawn on me that, what if, one of the gateways to the faery realm is through these wings… the beauty and wonder of nature is something that cannot fully be captured through words, only experienced personally. Even though I find myself stuck in a dark cloud in these confusing and frustrating times, a sense of Love was cultivated within me on this day spent with Mother Nature and looking into the tiny wings of the dragonfly.

The Rim

I set up a tent on the outskirts of the Garden

A patch that has escaped destruction and has maintained its

integrity.

The sighing Pines, tired from a long life of observing and growing quietly alongside their Mother.

It seems like these areas can be compared to man; it seems like more people are losing values and morals, and society is withering away in a self- preserving fashion.

It looks like it can be saved, but the core, the foundation, is disintegrating.

The false creators are watching this illusion slip through their fingers as quickly as it was formed in their minds.

I have pushed myself to the Rim of Existence

A little sliver of quiet land surrounded by innocent noise.

I am not sure what I am looking for, this place is free from man-made distractions and distortions

Just Mother and I

Wood and Green Leaf

Crunch of twigs and random serenity

Sigh of relief...

Soft surrender into the embrace of Unconditional Love

I hear their desperate calls

But this time, I cannot answer

The time has come

The Rim

August 15th: *I had a dream with my father, and we were in some sort of wilderness setting. We were travelling somewhere by foot and the terrain morphed from a woodland to an Iceland. The experience kind of reminded me of Boy Scouts when we used to go camping. We were going through the woods, I turned around and saw that there was a fairly tall but skinny grizzly bear sitting on the ground. I kept looking at the bear and when I looked him in the eye, he got up and started chasing us. For some reason I couldn't ignore the bear. It felt as if I was a little kid more, which made it feel even more like my Scout days. The bear started veering more towards my dad during this chase and he seemed to be having a little bit of fun with the bear, as if he wasn't afraid of being mangled. My dad tripped and fell on the ice once but got up before the bear could strike. I was trailing from behind and attempted to help by throwing things at the bear, which partially worked, but the bear was locked in on my father. We ended up on the top of a riverbed or lakebed that was frozen over, and the bear fell through the ice. I wanted to leave but my father wanted to make sure that the bear was alright. The thin grizzly ended up emerging from the water and got him/herself out, my father and*

I then advanced up the river. It was slippery so we had to be careful. On the tip of the hill, we could still see the bear down below. There were a bunch of ice crystals around us that lined a wall bordering us, it seemed then that we were in some sort of cavern or enclosed area with a lot of space. My dad had expressed the feeling that we were trapped atop the hill, but I showed him how we can advance. As we were inching along the wall trying not to slip, my dad started to collect the crystals that weren't cold, maybe they were quartz crystals. They were very fine and smooth. My dad was using them to distract the bear who was still slowly and ominously trailing behind us in the distance. I started collecting the crystals myself and putting them into my newfound sweatshirt kangaroo pocket. As we were reaching what seemed to be the end of the wall, we saw the bear behind us willingly jump into the now unfrozen lake/river. I looked closer and saw that there was now a large shell on the back of the bear. He swam to shore, and I noticed flipper arms now, the bear had transformed into a giant turtle! I told my dad that it was a turtle, a large turtle, and we went back to investigate. When we got to the bottom of the river/lakebed, my father kind of froze since he was the first one down and had more time to observe what was in front of us. Something was wrong. I looked at the turtle and saw that the shell was not real and was made from some sort of nylon/tent fabric to serve as an optical illusion, some sort of turtle suit.

Out of the suit emerged a native-looking man with a blow dart pipe in his hands. He was making occasional high-pitched noises, like a war chant, perhaps to keep the spirit-bear away. I slid down and behind my dad, who was still frozen in silent observation out of sight behind a boulder on the lake/riverbed. The native man meant no harm and from the other side of the boulder, he appeared telling me to use the darts on the bear if he comes back and presented me with a few long and sharp darts with different colored animal feathers tied to each dart. He then instructed me to put the darts into the blowgun in a specific way or else they will backfire somehow. I was asking deeper questions and then another native-looking man, seemingly older, came and sort of re-iterated the first native man's dart instructions. Interesting dream. Much love.

November 7th: *Light, Sun, Warmth... these are the states I wish to make my sanctuary, to become a beacon of light, defender to malevolent darkness, promoter of peace.*

I step onto the icy waters of uncertainty with the weight of a feather, feeling the kinetic energy enveloping my body. What is this feeling? Who are these people? I guess these questions may never be answered, maybe they don't need to be.

Who am I? What is my purpose? Why do I feel that I need a purpose, this burning force and desire? What is Love? Baby don't hurt me... don't hurt me... no more.

How pathetic, how childish, needing someone else.

This search will lead to the death of me, or maybe the birth? I

feel this urge to let go... what will come of me then?

Astral Investigations

I stared up at the blue sky… which was full of potential.

The clouds pass at a steady rate. Is the Earth spinning or is it just a current of wind swirling up above? Everything is being questioned in my mind.

So many people are sleeping… What should I do? For I cannot wake them.

Restlessness striking, wanting something to chew. Things are different than they once were and I have accepted this, but seeing the sleeping sheep around me that (for the most part) don't want to be woken up out of their slumber of ignorance and denial causes me some irritation. Or am I the one who is sleeping? Being God must be difficult and lonely… is that why we were created? The angels? My strong belief is that God (Infinite Creator, Unconditional Love) is operating within each of us, and we decide, with our Free Will, how this creative energy is translated. With that being said, there is no way of knowing for sure… which can bring us frustratingly back to square one on our journeys of experience and wisdom.

Due to being largely misled by the education system and like many others alike, I have no idea what I want or where I should direct my creative and restless energy, let alone recognizing and addressing this sleeping strength within. I have the desire to teach and assist children in ways in whic I wish I was taught and led, but do I have enough experience in the world and wisdom myself? I feel like a college degree does not substitute for experience and it seems like the best and wisest teachers are older and have been through the process of life through trial and error. These random thoughts and worries are scrambling through my mind… Why do I feel like I have to make a decision right now? Why are we so programmed to desire a career within this corrupted system?

This constant query naturally drew me to the study of the stars and the heavens, which is where we typically look when there are no other places to go: Astrology. Along with my two best friends, Pat and Michael, who are a keen set of musical brothers, literally and figuratively, took the dive into the abyss of inner-knowledge and understanding. There were many uncomfortable notions I have had towards the institution of modern religion. Astro theology, however, which is the beautiful fusion of Astrology and Theology (the study of God) as well as the study of the seven celestial bodies (Sun, Moon, Mars, Mercury, Venus, Saturn, Jupiter) and the tie between the various scriptures that mention the Saviour or 'Sun' of God, as well as the other various parallels with religion, which together create a package of understanding and insight that I had been searching for. A study that relates all major world religions, creating a sense of interconnectedness that has some profound simplicity to it.

These realizations encouraged me to want to shout from the rooftops and share the things I am learning before integrating and fully comprehending them myself. But as I was able to find out the hard way, many of the sheep live under a 'flock mentality and do not want to be educated and woken up. It ultimately is not my job to force someone's eyes open, however, I have found it effective to try to become an optimistic shepherd...

This study of Astro theology, if one is committed to self-knowledge and self-discovery, will become a natural way of life, which seems to be what turns the flock away from touching the subject due to the painful thought of diving into the deep and obscure well of the soul, for there is no guarantee of smooth passage. I have often turned away and denied many things that keep proving themselves as true in my life and keep bringing me back to the cycles of the heavens.

Societal programming has been effective in embedding fear into our psyche, through media and television and planned events, as well as toxic ways of living/thinking. This inquiry brings us to an interesting question: Are we really being programmed and how do we even notice? I will answer this question with another question, or perhaps a series of questions... Why do we see such a disconnect between people? Why do these many wealthy people who 'have it all' become morbid alcoholics and corrupted in order to get to cope with this level of psychopathy? Why is it so unclear and 'dream-like' to live a life of happiness? We notice by developing a sense of awareness and seeing the bubble of controlling factors once we begin to question everything; why things work the way they do in our society, what motivations may be behind fluoridating our drinking water and deceptions such as income taxes and the stock market.

We soon find out that most of our financial and political systems are connected and compartmentalized through a loose web of factors and people, all created by man to keep fellow man locked in a loop of confusion and oppression, chasing after bright lights. When everything on the outside becomes unbearable noise, I don't have any other effective option other than going within and cultivating a sanctuary and a healthy relationship with God and myself in order to truly learn...

12/09/15-

What a crazed and depraved state of mind that we have fallen into…

Every day it amazes me what I see in people's eyes; confusion mixed with happiness; horror sprinkled with joy. We often lose touch with and ignore that inner voice that allows us to remain tethered to our morals. I've learned in my short existence that we are all a part of a bigger design. Every person is a silky strand pertaining to a web of consciousness and of God, who is the spider; perfectly in tune and receptive of the vibrations that

When we are children, we often have the most imaginative and vivid dreams, some more vivid than others and there are some that stick with us throughout our whole lives, but it is interesting to think about what changes as we get older? It seems that we mostly dismiss this creative side of ourselves and turn to numbing out these sensations and emotions through drugs and alcohol or tv. However, this side of us cannot be killed without a fight and never truly goes away.

I started to become interested in the subconscious mind (the 'dream' aspect of the mind where we are not fully conscious or aware of but influences our actions and feelings and is a reflection of our conscious mind) as a guide and roadmap to understanding and completing my true self and nature. Through a few internet searches I came to the seemingly appropriate first step in my research, dream journaling. I have always enjoyed writing but have fallen off of the wagon for a bit, so I started documenting my dreams in order to identify any patterns, kind of like a cosmic stitching of my past, present, and future all in one in order to create a fluid and beautiful fabric.

Sometimes it is difficult to know where to begin, since there are those of us who do not enjoy writing and do not have, to our conscious recollection, any notable dreams. This seems to be a lie and a defense mechanism in order to avoid addressing our subconscious mind. I have found it useful to start writing down, to the best of ability, a dream or image that has been recurring throughout life or perhaps recently. The next step is to keep a pad of paper and a pen/pencil next to where you are sleeping (on the bed next to the pillow is fine) and attempt to write down the first thing that pops into the head when waking up. There are times in the middle of the night where I would have a clear dream-message come through and I will groggily and sloppily write it down and fall right back asleep. This is an experimentation and in no way will it be perfect, only through practice and the Will to Learn about oneself can we learn to stop comparing ourselves to others and locate our personal paths. Within time, you will begin to recall full dreams and write them down with more ease, as the bridge between your subconscious and conscious mind is formed and reinforced, allowing the creator(you) to walk freely back and forth (with awareness). I have disclosed a few personal entries that I have preserved over time for the enjoyment and reference of the dear reader:

04/22/17 12:50am EST-

I'm going to start the beginning of my journal with one of the

most vivid, relevant dreams I've ever had ...

It was a few nights ago, maybe it was May 17th or 18th and it

started in a car with my dad driving, me in the passenger seat,

my uncle Matt in the back, and my cousin Brett in the back as

well. We were driving through a wooded area and my uncle

was encouraging my dad to do some stunt with the car, my dad

being the younger brother gave into the encouragement, and

sent the car and us within, skidding off into a water/quicksand

covered ravine. None of us were injured and we were just

standing outside of the sinking car. My dad then pulled the car

out of the watery quicksand with one hand, like it was

weightless.

The dream then transitions to my mom's old apartment that she

shared with Bill in north Miami. My sister and I were alone,

and I was trying to call my parents on the phone, but they

wouldn't answer. I kept hearing the female automated voice

one hears when someone doesn't pick up the phone. After a few

more desperate tries, I began to grow paranoid of the voice for

some reason. I called again, and at the very end of the call,

there was a pause and then I heard the voice say, "we know",

which scared the daylights out of me, but it all seemed like a

normal part of the dream, and I went with it. I then looked outside and across the street from the apartment complex I saw

my mom and Grady, just looking at me blankly from across the

street, emotionless. My mom nudged Grady to run over to me,

which he did without emotion or hesitation. I jumped over the

edge from the 3rd floor on which we lived and scaled down

with poise and without hurting myself in order to retrieve

Grady. I picked him up and felt that he was pooping his pants

(he was around 3 or 4 at the time of the dream) but still showed

no emotion and didn't cry. I looked across to see my mom

getting picked up by a black van… which could symbolize a

dark force of some kind, that's how I felt about it, the rest is

fuzzy…

The beginning of my dream journalling was also during my probationary period, a.k.a. the darkest period of my life (so far) and a lot of buried emotions were coming to the surface through this practice. I had a therapist at the time as well who gave a pretty interesting analysis of my dream above, which was the only dream at the time that I could actively remember and has had an impact on me. She mentioned how, in the beginning, when my dad pulled the car out of the quicksand, that he represented strength and the 'hero' in my life and when the odds were against him, he pulled through. The scene with my sister and I alone in the apartment seems to symbolize my sister and I being alone through our parents' divorce and that I had to become firm in my ways. The scene with my mother telling Grady to come to me may be that she is giving up her joy and happiness in order to (wittingly or unwittingly) be swept away by this dark force (Bill). This interpretation, or at least hearing it from another person, almost brought me to tears. It showed me that our dreams are shadow reflections of our conscious lives, almost like a hidden teacher that presents fears, insecurities, and painful memories to us in order to address and correct them if we so choose. On the other hand, if we decide to ignore our inner self, this is why you see so much insecurity and abundance of bitterness in the streets.

So then, what changes as we get older? It seems that we bury our shadow selves and dismiss this side of us. Holly-wood and the 'fake media' have done a beautiful job at scaring the absolute daylights out of the people when it comes to understanding our subconscious 'shadow/mirror mind' through the fear of demonic possession, going insane, losing a false sense of security that we have clung so hard to and reinforced with our toxic genetically modified foods and alcohol in order to keep us dumb and quiet. When I begin to embrace the subconscious as a guidance and roadmap, the dreams started becoming more lucid and more symbolic', yet the only thing that truly changed was my perspective, since I now had a desire and motivation to brush the cobwebs and cockroaches off of this neglected side of myself. I highly recommend this practice, even if for a couple of days, they don't even have to be

consistent, which is what I seem to get caught up in (being a
Capricorn Sun I have a knack for structure and
consistency/repetition), as it seems that the scientific approach
works better for the study. Observing the images and people as
symbolic, rather than always literal, allows one to step back and
look at the 'big-picture' movie of one's life, one can also even
delve into past-life experiences (reference the Bhagavad-Gita
and similar eastern esoteric texts).

Once one familiarizes themself with symbols and how they
function, they start to appear everywhere and saturate our
'consumer' programming, buildings, company logos,
advertisements, etc.

It is shocking how many symbols and subconscious cues are
used to influence the general public. However, I don't think it
would be effective to turn this realization into a panic, but this
is where the real work started for me, for symbols take on the
power that we(man) give them, a game of energy and
magnetism if you will. Once the veil had started to slip off of
my eyes, I saw how much smoke and how many mirrors are
used to reflect the same ancient influential images on different
surfaces and colors and time periods while keeping everyone
bombarded with useless information and noise. The goal is
simple; cause a state of fear and disconnect among all people
and turn them against each other slowly and painfully.

It can't be that bad, can it? Look around, the air feels tense and compressed, like the Earth is holding her breath in anticipation of our decisions. But what do I know?

Distant Love

I don't always see her, but I feel her. Neither of us are in the space to receive each other. There is a veil between us, a screen that we agreed to create so that we can find each other again. In a different game, in a different life. There is no other option except to merge once again as one beautiful cosmic story. I have this weird feeling that I was meant to come and meet Calysta's mom with her. Since she lives in a different state and has her own demons with which she wrestles, Calysta doesn't see her much. I felt this strange connection with the two of them, misunderstood, beauty mixed with deceit and corruption. This common thread of pain and longing within their eyes that felt like home to me. Caly's mom let me borrow a book called 'Dark Places'. I have dreams sometimes that lead to them, this deep burning desire that can take hold of my entire mind, because I let it. I enjoy the role of the hopeless romantic, the dog in servitude to women. It seems like we want to be slaves to love, so shall it be.

(07/10/20, 5:58pm EST)-

I took a little post-work nap, it's been going really well, it's just hard adjusting to an office setting and re-acclimating to the ignorance in the world (I had been fired from my previous job for about 2-months, taxi driving in order to make money and to get out of the house, meaning that I was mostly to myself) around me. During my cat-nap I had a dream about something fascinating… I want to say it was some sort of mixture between Naruto (Japanese ninja cartoon) and Thor (old Nordic legend). I hate relating everything to movies and TV shows but I seem to have a close relation to the archetypes demonstrated in said movies and TV shows, as many do. I waited too long to write it down because I remained in a dazed, theta pondering state when I woke up and then thought about the single-file army of ants that are trying to break into my bedroom window. They're so resilient and hard-working, I almost feel like letting them get what they want… I want to live on my own, no restrictions, heal people, but it feels like I'm going through a necessary training, like a prerequisite in order to enter the true course. I digress, I pardon the interruption. I don't remember exactly what happened… I just remember the feeling of a lack of trust, a tension in the air. A dragon-like being had frozen solid right before my eyes, face snarled with teeth bared as if it was in mid attack but was stopped. Was it me who stopped the dragon? A deceptive plan perhaps? Things are changing out here.

__July 19th-__ What a mysterious and amazing life that we live. I had a dream that there was this evil force. An unbeatable, deep-rooted, evil force that was able to conquer the power of Love and Compassion. I struggle to accept that love can have a tangible, physical power, as I am under constant spiritual attack under the guise of being malnourished, mentally unstable, and the whole spectrum of resistance. I remember a spider-represented entity. It secreted these web-like tendrils that could find you wherever you were, as it was after the strong-willed and the just, with the sole purpose of corrupting and tainting the power of Good. As these slow, creeping tendrils fastened themselves onto my hands, as darkness was taking me over, cell-by-cell, I was completely still with my thoughts and then completely regained control after I thought about everyone I loved having my back and putting a hand on my shoulder. The tendrils recoiled and were forced off through the power of Divine Love. I then remember keeping the darkness trapped in this rolled up rug that was laid before me. The rug was bubbling with green anger and trying to regain its power through fear and uncertainty, but I was certain that this entity would be sealed in the name of Love. I ended up transforming the rug into a scroll, which told the tale of the encounter and battle, to be sealed away until the next incarnate of evil were to have the will and audacity to offer the world a *needed lesson. When all hope seems to be lost. We are vessels carrying angels, if we listen to the call and accept the mission.*

Clearing (07/24/20)-

I have been having consistent breakthroughs in the Astral realm. This may be because I have been making a lot of conscious changes in order to make room for the Divine work. I receive these amazing moments of clarity from my dreams as I let them flow with intention, but without a specific expectation in mind: a conscious observer. I am no longer secretly obsessed over Calysta, I am not as angry and bitter towards the world and the 'system', it just feels good to be alive. Being a Saturn-ruled sun (Capricorn), I am very involved with time and limitations, structure and discipline and have been trained to heavily abide by this through my father.

I don't know where God and the Universe will take me, but I need to stop making hasty decisions based on impulse. What do I want? Or what does God want for me? Forget about the money. As we are perplexed that Plato and Porphyry could spend their lives in contemplation without the need to make money. There must be some disconnect between then and now, ancient Greece and modern America, for philosophy is practically dead. It has been mutated into a form of 'Insta-Spam' and 'Facehook' that contains watered-down, half-cocked views of the small world they live in. I would like to help restore the beauty and integrity that once filled the minds of men and women, and I believe it lies sleeping within us.

Stay Aware, Much Love

-Zeal

June 29th- *It started with me clocking into a futuristic corporate-like job and I was surrounded by a bunch of robot-like workers who seemed to be stuck in the same cycle. I was in line with someone who appeared to be a future friend, someone I haven't met yet. It felt much like what I imagined 'A Brave New World' by Huxley to be like. I went up to the second floor by elevator and I walked into an ominous scene that made me feel like I walked into a horror scene from a film. I walked into a classroom where a black man stormed in right after me with a gun and started shooting at people in the classroom, he was very angry and demented. I don't know if I got shot or if I was merely spectating, almost as if I were sent back in time to prevent the event from happening. I was then sent forward back into what felt like an investigation of the black man in order to see what the motives were. It appears that the man was framed by a couple of race-war starters who planted something in his house. It turns out I was with my two friends, Linguini and Barbosa, who were my partners in removing the evidence from* *the property that would further incriminate the shooter. We ended up riding away in these weird flying chariots doing some crazy aerial maneuvers with ease. The dream transitioned into a scene with my dad sleeping on the couch and I walked in late at night and my dad was talking to me in his sleep. He was giving me tips on my motor scooter that I was driving at the time, mentioning that he 'doesn't press the gas down all the way'. I was also eating a fruit that tastes like a peach/nectarine and it also had a pit in the center. The rest is fuzzy.*

July 3rd- *I don't really know how it started, but I found myself underwater with members of my family. It seemed like we were diving together, but we didn't have snorkels or gas tanks. I felt fear as I was in the ocean because I couldn't see anything around me until my mom motioned to put on my glasses underwater. After swimming aimlessly for a while, I suddenly felt the need to come up for air. As I rose to the surface, I felt the energy of the ocean around me and I wasn't scared despite the immense power of the ocean. I saw the vast horizon and nearby on the water's surface I saw a gray fin slice through and became frightened. I went underwater and put on my glasses (not goggles) so I could get a good look at the shark, which turned out to be a hammerhead. I then tried to flee from the shark after touching its belly, it still scared me, maybe representing fear in my life. I swam over to a patch of rock that appeared and stood on it. In every cardinal direction I could* *see a different scene with a different landscape. To the north I saw a lit-up, dystopian, industrialized city, to the east I saw a half-buried, underwater city. The rest is fuzzy.*

August 23rd, 2017: *I had a dream the other night that keeps re-circulating in my head. The whole thing is blurry and hard to make out, probably because I smoked pot the night of the dream, so my brain was a little hazy. The part that keeps passing back and forth is a scene where I saw a yearbook-like photo of myself and beneath the photo where the name should go, I see 'Rosicrucian'. I'm not sure if it was a subconscious association with Rosicrucianism through loose family ties, or if it was part of my wish fulfillment of being part of a protected school of thought and culture. I have this underlying delusion that my family is more relevant than I have been led to believe. I'm sure many people have these hopes and curiosities, but my imagination runs wild with it. The interesting synchronicity and significance of the dream at the time was that I woke up at Chris' place and saw a book that belonged to my friend Cameron's dad, which was left at the beacon. The title consisted of a sequence of words including 'Masonry, Kabbalism, and Rosicrucianism'.*

(07/11/19)- I have been digging up a lot of my suppressed memories, I want everything to be cleared upon the time of ascension/harvest. I was at the Japanese garden for a solid 2.5-3 hours just meditating on everything in its raw form in the presence of Nature. How it is such a blessing to have moved so close to this beautiful place. I'm not sure what exactly has changed, but it has. I'm painfully committed to my spiritual growth and nothing else is really important to me right now. People's true intentions seem to stand out with more of an alarm, or is it me projecting my insecurities? Oftentimes I feel confused about what to do, what moves to make. I have bonds on this Earth that are hard for me to break, chiefly the bond I have with my little half-brother, Grady. 'Just a little longer' I tell myself, at least until he's a certain age... I can't leave him completely alone with my mom and Bill. How dare they bring such innocence into the world and show how corrupt the world can be so early in life, like having a child is the new marriage-saver. I at least want to plant a seed of unconditional love and help nurture his communication with God and his Higher Self. He must be scared sometimes, like I was. There is so much that's wrong... that needs to be put into place, it seems. I've realized (painfully) that I can't be the person to do that alone, but I surely can help, on whatever scale that may be. Shit is crazy out here; I'm dropping my friends like flies, having racing thoughts and desires, crying like a little girl sometimes.

However, it all feels like a shedding of a past skin and growing out of a lower form of density and thought.

December 11th- 'Spiritual Warfare':

I wake up often feeling like I went to a lot of places which ends up making me more tired than when I went to sleep. This entertains the idea that we travel between dimensions and realities as we are in the dream realm. What is most important in life? Money? Love? Recognition? Love is something that can melt the ice that builds up in the soul and break down barriers, allowing people to work together. There is a massive absence of truth in the world that many people don't realize, I don't understand to the full degree. I have been keeping away from a lot of 'conspiracy' information in fear of getting wrapped into the flurry of misinformation or 'fake news'. I can't deny that we are spiritual warriors that have been drafted into this world, for we are in a time of spiritual awakening..

January 26th: 'New Priorities'- *As I continue to study the self and the occult (hidden" knowledge that has been shielded from ignorant and sleeping eyes, things begin to shift perspective* *and degrees of importance. Addictions are more conquerable, decisions are clearer. One stops being a slave to the mind and body, since minds and body are not God, but parts of God's creation. I struggle with lust, for I am easily wooed and fascinated by the female form and aesthetic. Having vices in mind, I must not treat them as special because this, in turn, gives them more power and form, the fantasy that I am some Dr. Jekyll/Mr. Hyde that can't control the animal. I continue to accept that I can't control life, but I am in control of choosing how the creation flows through me, showing that love and true knowledge is not for a particular race, creed, or background, but a divine right granted to all people who agree to accept the truth. We must remember that we are the power behind our governments, we have the ultimate say on how the country should be run. Sadly, the 'powers-that-be' tirelessly and patiently make sure that certain classes of people are as separated, judgmental, and ignorant as possible. Not to mention addicted to comfort, security, and Sunday Night Football. Although corruption and evil seem to be rampant in society, there are positive forces seeing to it that we will overturn and remodel this wretched financial system that has been embedded into the world for quite some time. I don't see the need to fight physically or shed any more blood, as hatred breeds hatred. I am a firm believer that we change the world by changing ourselves, and by doing this, the change begins to take hold within the collective. Take my hand, join me on this dance. for evil does not stand a chance. Much Love.*

May 6th, 'Depth'- *I am beginning to think that the depth that I am so passionately attracted to displaying to the public, may have a form of illusory deceit laced within. Grand explanations for the divine are unnecessary. I get bombarded by these thoughts and complex algorithms of shapes and energy that seem to help me unlock the true path, but I also feel like I don't have to peel back so many layers so quickly. Due to the doubt, stagnation and environmental pressures, I have been called to question my heart in a vicious cycle of thoughts. Thankfully I have the bigger picture in the background, while the deceit and materialism fade along with the disturbing noise. Much love,*

Stay tuned.

Unceasing (3:30am EST)- *I had this noteworthy dream where I was crossing a street, a highway sizzling and buzzing with cars, however, I was not scared. It was a moment where all forces were in harmony to help me cross that street, as long as I was willing to step out of my own way. Some old man, possibly my dad, or a representation of my higher self. Without an expression or further hesitation, I dodged every car and with patience and poise. I crossed the busy street. Objective clarity. Perseverance of Luke.*

The Ambassador

Alexander Azoth was born to a mysterious family, well-known and liked, but obscure. Not much has been established on John Azoth, Alex's father, other than that he was a hardworking, hard-laughing German Avocado farmer who one day appeared in the Southeast of the United States...

The common story is that John migrated with his mouse-like yet firm and warm-hearted wife Lori, from somewhere in Germany. Their generation comes from an era of barbarism and stubborn persecution of free thought and free speech; meaning the intelligent and common-sensical had to hide their thoughts or think on their feet in order to maintain and incorporate this suppressed Truth and Love into society without getting jailed, exiled or killed. The ones who followed the quota of mindless obedience and ignorance were promoted to teachers, military generals, CEOs of businesses in order to spark and steady the military intervention and implement the military-industrial complex that has its tentacles worked into all branches of the world governments today. John Azoth fell somewhere in the middle of all of this, he saw destiny and opportunity within the settling embers of World War II. Big John Azoth, standing at a tall, but firm 6'3" and 165 pounds was a jack-of-all-trades, if you will. He wasn't committed to any specific line of work, although particularly fond of poetry and avocados. Poetry was a way for John to express his true beliefs and feelings in a suppressed society, if only he could get his poems to people who wanted them or needed them. He believed that poetry and avocados would bring peace to the world, in one way or another. It was one of those childish dreams that never went away.

Big John Azoth served in WWII as a volunteer medic and civilian scientist, assisting the hospitals with x-ray technology and eventually began developing radar technology along with various groups of military 'professional' scientists. The reason John was able to keep up with and even surpass many of these learned men was that he was ahead of his time in analysis and intuitive thinking, John simply understood how things worked at a simple glance and had a childlike curiosity to find out how they played into a grander operation.

By the time the war had ended, John had served his country and learned how much he despised war and the bloodthirsty barbarism behind the ordeal. Through working on radar, John had overheard technicians and the occasional decorated generals who carelessly mentioned how 'we need war' and 'the world would be chaos without war' with gritted yellow teeth and the look of bloodlust in their eyes. A lot of them would like to watch the world burn and use the shiny big toys that can get the job done. Instead of directing our heat-seeking missiles of blame on the war generals, we must remember that this complex, that trains and indoctrinates eager-to-serve- men into becoming trigger-squeezing dogs, has developed over time into the confusion that has sprouted today. In the time of the War, however, a lot of these original punches were thrown. Recruiting Germany's top scientists of all fields in order to help the government control and manipulate their people with the vast arm of Goebbels' infamous propaganda. John Azoth wanted nothing to do with this. He wanted to take Lori and create something that wasn't clouded by soot and blood and shiny black boots and run as far away from this smile less, colorless way of life as God would permit. He wanted to go to America.

John had been married to Elora (Lori) since 1933 (before the war) and were rather reserved towards each other, most likely due to observing *their* parents barely touching each other, but seemingly had a deep love and faith towards one another. However, after the war came to a halt, John and Lori held each other tight and cherished their blossoming relationship.

Lori was skeptical about leaving Germany, but a feeling in the pit of her stomach wouldn't allow her to pass up the opportunity. That, and the look in John's eye made her feel like he would be going with or without her. John was a determined

man, and John and Lori Azoth were both cycle-breakers.

"What would we do there?" was Lori's first and only question.

John looked her straight in both of her eyes with a warm and

reassuring smile, "We'll start an avocado farm".

Extracted from: *John Azoth's Collection of Poems:*

Lifting Fog

I have a deep-rooted passion within my Soul.

I wake up in fear and anger, for I have never been truly taught

how to deal with these emotions.

However, through time, I have been able to connect with

nature and with God, learning that we always have the power

within us

To rise

To fall

To love from a distance

to feel…

I sometimes wake up in terror

But as of late, I have been fortunate to look observe from

outside of myself

Through the eyes of God

This terror isn't me, it is not real

I strive to relinquish my fear and anger

replacing them with love and compassion

And so, it is …

On March 21st of 1946, with the little money that John and Lori Azoth had after the war, they took a freighter ship to New York, USA, the 'Grail of Hope and Opportunity'. John didn't enjoy New York … too noisy and predictable, Lori felt the same way. They had already set their sights on a plot of land in Miami, Florida (the weather there is more suitable for Hass Avocados).

Many ambitious, anxious, and battle-ridden Hope Seekers gathered from all over the world and funneled into ports such as those of New York, Canada, California and Florida in order to start anew. John and Lori weren't the only couple seeking to farm with little experience. However, if you remember, John Azoth was a jack-of-all-trades … and a quick learner. While people were mesmerized by the bright lights and the newfound freedom, John was mapping in his head what he was going to do and where he needed to apply more of his focus and energy. He also didn't come to America completely unequipped, and neither did Lori. John was somewhat of a flatterer at times and, on the freighter to America, developed a friendly relationship with a stocky Irish landlord who was looking to sell 12 acres of land that John and Lori just so happened to be headed towards. Lori, the quiet genius, knew of a soil fertilizer that can turn virtually any type of soil into a fertile Garden of Eden. This miracle mineral is a mono-atomic gold powder that converts the sun's energy into a resurrecting/rejuvenating agent that brings the soil to its optimal state. All that was left was to get to work, John could barely sit still. Along with the entrepreneurs, there were many immigrants looking to work anywhere they could, which also made farm-labor not so difficult to come by for John and Lori, especially with the warmth and hope that radiated from the pair while also awakening these faculties within others, these people may even have worked for free.

John and Lori Azoth arrived at their small, cozy farmhouse that was made of old cedarwood but appeared surprisingly vibrant and sturdy. The 12 acres weren't a whole lot, but John marveled at this land like a little child marveling at the beauty of a free-running stallion or perhaps a seamstress marveling at a dazzling silk fabric that can only be found in the secluded mountains of Japan. The amount of care and love that John and

Lori put into their small avocado farm, coupled with their kind-hearted nature towards the mixture of Irish and Polish workers that they had working with them, caught the eye of the rapidly growing community. There was no other way.

About a year into John and Lori's 'New Life', on a Christmas evening, they had a baby. A son. Little Alexander Azoth. Although poor Lori wailed like a sailor, the baby boy did not cry during birth, as if he were reluctantly expecting to be born. Little Alexander grew up keen and inquisitive, constantly tiring John's patient ear with his barrage of questions. Lori, the mother, primarily educated Alex while John and his friends worked on the farm during the day, and she was well aware of his swift development and inquiring nature. Lori would watch in a playful and silent delight at the sight of John's scrunched brow as young Alex would confound his father with his dazzling young mind.

The Miami townsfolk would frequently visit the Azoth Avocado farm, which was kindly open to the public, yet there was a kind of reverence and respect towards the Azoth family and people never stole from the farm, they simply enjoyed coming over just to chat with Lori and Alex or watch Big John plowing the fields and gazing up towards the warm orange sun setting in the West, with his look of determination and admirations towards the beauty and possibilities of Life.

By the time that Alex had turned 14, John and Lori understood well before then that their son had the same, if not more, ambition and determination as his parents, and may eventually want to leave the farm and embark on his own journey and follow his heart. Lori taught Alex how to read a map and understand how to navigate with a compass, as well as being able to use the sun and the stars as reference (there is a lot more to Lori than meets the eye). John, the father, taught young and eager Alex how to gather wild plants and which berries are safe to eat and what their medicinal properties are, as well as which ones will kill him. John also taught his son how to hunt and trap wild game if necessary. Alex has grown into a handsome young man, with a shiny mop of golden blonde hair and penetrating blue eyes that naturally caused strangers who encountered him to walk on eggshells, as if he instantly saw their lies and insecurities, which Alex wouldn't take interest in anyway.

Alexander Azoth did not like to argue, but he also did not like to be wrong. He had a stubborn arrogance to him that was common among kids his age, however, Alex wielded this arrogance with a humility and stubbornness that made it seem that he was defending some larger Truth that couldn't quite be explained, it was just worth defending, sometimes irrationally and to destructive ends. Alex would stick up for the 'weak person' that was getting ganged up on and ridiculed or bullied by some even more insecure and disturbed charlatans, which sometimes ended in a black eye or split lip after a heated skirmish.

He would engage in deep and dreamy conversations with people he met that day and never see them again. There was this air of compassion and love that went along with the Azoth family, some people despised it, mostly because they didn't understand what they felt, but most saw this quality and energy as a blessing and a 'breath of fresh air', for they were a humble folk that seemed to only care to cultivate love and peace … as well as tasty rich Hass avocados!

It wasn't that the Azoth family had possessed something that the rest didn't, or some complex set of factors that placed them above the rest. The Azoth family simply moved forward by the guidance within their heart's, their God-given guidance, and the Universal Truth that anything is possible when one is authentic and genuine to oneself and those around them... They were an inspiration within the community.

They had their ups and downs just like any other family, they just skipped the petty fights and pouts and lo! The dark cloud passed right over the Azoth farm without stopping, for they did not feed negativity. There was no time or energy to be wasted on such a thing...

Little Alex had even bigger ambitions than his father, but not

for the material world, for the internal and spiritual world that

directly reflected the material, a balance that was clearly calling

to Alex ever so softly, yet consistently, throughout his young

life, as if he had some crinkled-up destiny that needed

unfolding. There was this golden wonder to the boy that

sparked either love or fear in people, rarely ever in between,

which inspired him to spend a lot of time alone, saddening

young Alex at times. For he was a rather serious person, born in

the heart of winter, Alexander Azoth had the stoic coldness of a

loyal soldier. This could all be found in his glance, his energy.

Growing Pains (1933)

It is confusing, growing up through this Life

We think we know, but we know not

Not until we try…

We fall and grow frustrated and bitter, yet we keep going

For we have a loving hand guiding us

Ever so lightly, yet firm.

Friends and family give good counsel

But not like that of the Lord within

The True voice and the fire to fight sin

That burns and yearns to know God, whatever that means.

We grow, slowly, sometimes to quickly

Faith and Love is what has been missing

They will scoff and disagree, but behind the veil of the Ego

They too feel the growing pains

Which only God can soothe.

-John Azoth's Collection of Poems

Even with all of these seemingly infallible qualities and charming personality, Alex yearned to connect with people for some reason. He knew that things would be a lot more convenient if he didn't feel this way, but there was an uneasiness that constantly surfaced in between his moments of joyful isolation and playful family laughter. A disorienting sense of hopelessness. He frequently had the feeling that he needed to be doing something for himself or for others, yet he was 14 years old and didn't understand much about himself! Young Alex had this strange feeling that he wasn't 'good enough' to be happy. This feeling scared Alex and he kept this secret locked away along with his multiplying passions and emotions. His parents were innovative and amazing, but they were simple and tired folk. They have come a long way and were happy where they were, and Alex didn't want to cause any problems. He couldn't imagine disrupting the seemingly perfect image of a happy, well-reputed avocado family. Alex secretly began to resent it all. He felt as if he were stolen from a different time in a parallel star system and was forced or fooled into incarnating on this Earth, some strange feeling of disconnect.

The only person that Alex dared tell his 'secrets' to be his indifferent and possibly even more stubborn best friend, Eric, who was the same age as Alex (born 33 days earlier) and came from a migrant Irish family who kept to themselves but possessed the seemingly rare traits of loyal friendship and common sense. Alex could share anything with Eric because of that very stubbornness and indifference, things would go into one ear and out the other, but Eric somehow extracted the 'nutrients' (which is how he described it) from the conversation which seemed to dance alongside the symphony playing inside of his head. Eric was a musician; he could play the guitar in such a way that it even inspired Alex to want to take up guitar from time to time. Eric would play and Alex would sing, nothing in particular, they simply flowed together through the medium of music and art. Eric possessed vision and confidence, which Alex sought to cultivate within himself, while Alex possessed deep emotion and empathy, which Eric didn't seem to care much about, but served as a natural balance to his own energy. The two young men supported each other in a growing society of materialism and willful ignorance; folks wanted to escape the poverty and desolation of war and America had naturally become a distant symbol for peace and new beginnings. However, folks are beginning to lose sight of why we came in the first place, with a new wave of competition over land and greedy demons hatching in people's hearts.

Alex and Eric would go on long walks along the Azoth farm and the surrounding creeks and marshlands as well as the countryside and get lost in deep thought and conversation. They would find themselves again when they became hungry or thirsty, or when one or both of their legs started to cramp up.

Eric's passion was music, Alex's was poetry, and together, they

were a dream in the works.

Catharsis- *Surrounded by darkness*

filled with anger

But on the horizon of the soul, a dazzling light so pure

The saviour has been born

For the human race

A release of Death and Youth

On our paths we ride, unsure of the proper pace

Together we find the Key

"I'm sick of this". Alex muttered to Eric after a long period of silent nature walking one sunny afternoon, they took a seat on the rim of a small pond outside of the Azoth farm.

"Sick of what?" chiseled Eric. He knew what Alex was talking about, he just wanted to hear Alex say it.

"All of this; the faking, the material life everyone is so quick to lose themselves to… all people seem to care about are *things*. Nobody cares about love, morals, and integrity. Piety is dead. Money and Power have become our Gods". Alex let the sentence out with relief, as if he were holding in a sneeze. Eric let a satisfied smirk sprout slightly, "What are you gonna do about it?"

This simple yet puzzling question caused Alex to pause for a short while and really think of his answer, for he never really knew the effect that someone else asking the question could pose on him. After a couple of long thought-filled minutes, Alex shared what he had formulated, "I don't think there's much I can really do for the whole situation, but I can follow my own path with integrity and liberate myself from this mental prison. This endless repetition of war and the following intellectual and economic trauma. People have inevitably become complacent, comfortable with their false sense of security and mental slavery. They even defend it! I guess, I can only do my best at fulfilling my destiny. Where will that lead me? That isn't up to me ultimately. But I wouldn't have such strong feelings about it if it didn't have at least *some* inkling of truth, you know?"

Alex wasn't sure if Eric truly listened to a word he said, he often wore a blank 'nobody home' look on his face. Like he has learned to check out of reality for however long he pleases, maybe it is his form of escape and defense in this loud and noisy 'new' world. However, Eric did ask those simple questions that Alex hadn't actually laid out and analyzed himself, which ultimately got the job done. Conversely, Alex would provide the self-analysis template that Eric seemed to disregard and be too lazy or carefree to address. They balanced each other out.

"You need to relax, Al". Eric said with a half-baked sympathetic grin. As mentioned previously, indifferent and stubborn. On the other hand, Eric stayed true to himself and those who were close to him. This authenticity seemed to quickly be fading in 1950s America. Young Alex wanted to remain true to himself and others. There was no other way...

A few nights later, Alex had a dream. It was a blessed dream sprinkled with a Divine Touch. Alex saw himself, as if he were floating above and observing with God's eye, speaking at a podium with an emblem or logo emblazoned in gold on the front and both side panels of the podium. The emblem or logo was blurry (possibly blurred out intentionally?) and Alex couldn't make it out in his current spectator state. The version of himself that he was observing was older, same golden-blonde hair, but slightly darker at the roots, and the gold had shifted and was naturally highlighted on different parts of the head, giving the appearance of thin gold feathers scattered along his head. There was a mass wave of people in attendance, it was breathtaking. Barely any space between each person, there must have been tens of thousands. Alex watched himself in silent amazement and curiosity, there was a sort of warmth that was generating in the seat of his chest, a sort of icy-hot longing...

Alex's older, evolved version was gazing over the ruckus with his bald eagle stare, it seemed like he was individually scanning the crowd with patience or maybe just waiting patiently and

gracefully for the noise to die down so he could speak. Future

Alex seemed serious.

Once the blob of people became quiet enough to allow him to

speak,

"My friends... my family..." His voice sounded a little huskier
and exhausted, but warm and deep. "The day is upon us...
where we must stand up for our liberty... There is an evil
among us that takes on many forms in order to suit its specific
interests, which is to destroy love and unity and enforce fear
and disconnect... This evil will infect people and convince them
to lie, kill, cheat, and steal in order to paralyze all of us
through fear and ignorance, as well as denial of the plain
Truth; that this world is for all of us, this government created
by the People in order to serve the People... Somewhere along
the way this message has seemed to be lost in translation, and
we have allowed ourselves to become slaves to debts and
diseases of the Mind" ... Future Alex took a brief pause to look

over the crowd once again, as if he were acknowledging each

of them individually, and the crowd remained silent. They truly

believed in him and the energy was united. Future Alex

proceeded:

"We have all struggled and have unconsciously fed this dark
system in one way or another for far too long. It is time that we

wake up and work together and experience destiny together

through Truth, Love, and Compassion through God. The

Father, Son, and Holy Spirit. The trinity that men and women

must find within themselves and that has kept truly great

nations from falling into lust, corruption and loss of faith in

God and each other." This concluded Alex Azoth's dream speech. The crowd was going nuts. Real-time Alex was yanked out of his third-person view and sprung straight up in his bed with a sharp gasp and bulging blue eyes. He simply stared forward at his closed bedroom door and felt a sense of determination that he had never felt before. This feeling of standing up and fighting for suppressed and hidden Truth, this Truth that was bigger than him and even the Azoth Avocado farm, which at this point had expanded to 200 acres (Big John has been busy), bigger than Big John Azoth himself! This dream, that night, is what helped spark Ambassador Alexander Azoth.

Alex ended up leaving on his journey 3 years later, at the transformative age of 17, in order to experience and observe the world and be able to write about it and perform personal studies so that he can relate to things and learn. He had a long-heartfelt conversation with his parents, John and Lori, about how he truly felt and what was on his mind. John and Lori were expecting this in their bright young man sooner or later but enjoyed and delighted at the puffed chest that Alex had created in order to 'break the news'. The three of them sat around a campfire that they liked to tell stories over, the tales seem to come to life and dance over the flames along with the floating embers and sound of the rustling fields. Lori and Alex usually listened in attentive love to John's plentiful and imaginative stories.

Lori knew Alex best of all, for she was the mother and had a direct link to his heart and emotions, even though faint and subtle, Lori was an intuitive and caring woman. John, although naturally scared and sad to hear that his young boy has the Wanderer Spirit, the restless spirit, he nonetheless accepted that Alex was a piece of him and a piece of God, who needs to explore, to fulfill itself through something great and beautiful. There was no other way.

John silently walked into the old cedar farmhouse (slightly more aged at this time but the warm appearance and energy had been maintained) and came back out a couple minutes later with a leathery piece of paper gently in hand that seemed to be at risk of crumbling into dust if dropped or handled too roughly.

John slowly sat down without breaking eye contact with the old paper, then slowly looked up at Alex with a warm, reassuring grin, "Whenever you get lost and are in need of love and guidance, which you will from time to time, here is my most prized possession." John playfully chuckled, "I would say my most prized possessions are you and your mother, but I don't own either of you." Big John Azoth's eyes sparkled at his wife and son, who were sitting next to each other by the fire. "This is a poem passed down to me from my father, and he from his, and I leave it to you." John handed the paper delicately but with intention to young Alex, who tried to mirror the delicacy and purpose that his father showed towards the old family relic. Alex cherished the heirloom and kept it with him wherever he went. Even through weather and travel and time, the poem survived, as if protected by a Higher Spirit, in order to be delivered for a Higher Purpose.

The New War

The buzzing has grown louder than before... I don't like that feeling. Things have appeared steady, but they are shaking at the foundation, as there is a battle behind the curtain, a war on emotion and thought. It's strange because when the day you think you're waiting for finally arrives, what comes next? There is a sobering moment where things aren't crystal clear, there seems to be no plan. There is a subtle despair in the air, while I look up to the gray sky, which seems to reflect my mood and mental state. The economy is crashing as people have been losing their jobs and slowly losing their sanity, which may be necessary in order to finally wake up. There have been these 'blackouts' that occur around 3-4 times a day, which cause every organic being (or so they say) to go into a catatonic state which has affected people in different ways according to their biology; some have died, some have developed nervous disorders that don't allow them to sit still, along with other nervous disorders, but the majority go into a seizure. The 'professionals' have their heads lodged up their asses dealing with the politics of the medical industry and the select money mafia that has the medical mafia and their promoters on speed-dial. It runs deep. The unpredictability of the blackouts has made it difficult for most people to work and, with the economy crashing, people are receiving government checks in order to pacify them into mindlessness and government dependency.

The local governments have been enforced to install padding into everyone's home (who can afford it or who are willing to sign up for life-long 'padding insurance') so that nobody cracks their heads open or what have you during the blackout periods (which is happening around the world, inspiring the initiative). This also implies that those who cannot afford the padding have to come up with their own ways of protection. The blackouts started around 6 months ago, coincidentally around the time when President Puppe assumed office of the U.S. through a 'mail-in' voting system, where millions of votes were changed from Ambassador Azoth to Puppe overnight. Nobody has seen the President give any public addresses or appearances since he assumed office.

Many theories have erupted for the cause of these worldwide 'blackouts'. One being that God has blessed us with a reset from work and financial life and gives us time to enjoy our government benefits and our newly implemented 'social credit system', which is scheduled to replace social security and most forms of physical identification and finance. The other main, yet more controversial, theory is that there are strong EMP (Electro-Magnetic Pulse) devices located strategically at different points on the Earth and are set to a calculated but irregular schedule to send out the pulses that us 'sheep' experience. Since our hearts are primarily magnetic and our brains primarily electric, these pulses interfere with normal brain function and frequency, forcing the brain and nervous system into the catatonic state mentioned previously. This theory, although grounded in a more Earthly and cynical harness, can be fused with the first theory involving God, for is God not in all things? However, the latter theory has been coined by 'conspiracy theorists' who have learned to watch what they say around the ignorant and uninformed, much like our friends during World War II...

The end goal, it is rumored and gathered through different channels of intel, behind the EMP theory would be that the same money/power mafia matrix that funds the medical industry would gather in these 'safe zones' where they are protected and unaffected by the blackouts and use these windows of time to further advance their schemes, as they feed on the chaos and fear. Why would they need/want to do this? Another great question! Because the 'general public' has started to wake up and smell the figurative coffee, not allowing this blatant government takeover.

Local governments, however, have issued a 'stay-at-home' curfew mandate until further notice, causing isolation anxiety and a cut-off from socializing and relating with others on the blatant lies and madness. However, as the heat of the fire rises, there is a resistance within the People's hearts that overpower the money mafia with Divine Justice. There are information channels that have been created in order to directly expose these mobsters, who are getting arrested behind the scenes by the busload. The murky swamp is being drained. I have become a firm believer in striving towards the balance of energies in the Universe(uni-verse), a yin and yang if you will. What we see on the te(lie)vision and the mainstream (and even some alternative) media is the desperate attempt to confuse the public and force certain narratives.

The heads of the National Medical Organization talk about a 'cure' being created for the blackout effects and even a microchip installment in the back of the skull in order to prevent the blackouts 'entirely'. The progressive and paid-off scientists are foaming at the mouth to create this technology, with their curious minds being used against them and their country. This is similar to post WWII when the German scientists were funneled into America (Project Paperclip) in order to create innovations in the new country (look into the origins of Werner Von Braun of NASA and Walt Disney of the Disney dynasty).

This all seems doom and gloom, this is the Truth. Yet, there are good people with love in their heart and soul within the government that have been working through enemy lines in order to use this 'big move' against them. Ambassador Azoth (our former leader who was basically forced out of office by the opposing party) has been swimming against the strong current of evil and corruption, serving as the patriot and balance that we have called for. Azoth has busted countless pedophile rings, satanic blood cults, and different forms of cockroaches who operate in the dark. However, many people doubt our leader and I have had my doubts as well, nobody is perfect, but there was this epiphany or vision that I experienced while walking along the rim of a pond one day during a beautiful sunset. It felt like I had been there before: **I was talking with Ambassador Azoth in a limousine. I don't remember what either of us were saying up to that point, but it felt strange that this dream was so clear. The only words I do recollect the Ambassador saying were, "Nice** talking to you, gotta go!" and he vanished. I looked out of the windshield from the back seat of the limo and there was this figure wearing a futuristic, gas mask-looking helmet that fit tight to the head and face. He was also holding a futuristic paintball-looking device that seemed to be a gun or laser scanner, pointing it straight at my face. I looked through the laser, which stretched to me through the windshield and the limo, like a moth to a flame, it was a mesmerizing infrared laser. I saw where the laser came from; three consecutive, horizontal, glowing x's at the end of the barrel of the gun that sent out three beams (one from each 'x') that converged into one laser that reached me at the back of the limo. The rest is fuzzy, almost like I got my memory wiped (End of dream).

I know what you're thinking: 'how can you build any case off of a dream like that?', to this, I would answer with another question or two: How did any great inventor receive a great idea through their dreams? How did the apostles and prophets of the Bible, or any sacred religious text for that matter, receive their communes with God? The unconscious mind and the Pineal gland (third eye) have a lot more correlation and influence on the physical world than we think. When one pays attention and studies the patterns of time and the conscious and unconscious 'cues' in the physical world, one can see these moves from afar, like a big chess game.

When one goes on solitary walks in nature and around flowing

bodies of water these revelations tend to be confirmed as well,

through piercing emotion and mental clarity that is unmatched

in the material world. I seek to understand the chess game like

Bobby Fischer. My favorite psychologist, Carl Jung, made it a

mission of his to explore the shadow side of the self, the

unconscious 'shadow' mind, so that he can truly guide people

into becoming their own personal psychologists and guides,

with aims to inspire the troubled to join in holy matrimony with

the Father(God), the Sun(You) and the Holy Spirit(the

Aether/fluid electric potential that flows all around us and

through us, and through which God and the Angels can

communicate with us), which, I feel, is the end goal for any

True psychologist. The ones who give you little nuggets of

truth in order to keep you coming back are scam artists using

their degrees to perpetuate a career, which is far from the Truth.

However, it seems like many psychologists DO care, but we are

erring humans and the ones who are attracted to psychology

seem to require a little imperfection themselves in order to be

effective and relatable, maybe not.

I have been drawn to isolation. Not sure if it is good or bad, since my perspective of 'good' and 'bad' has drastically changed over the past couple of years. I see that the 'bad' and 'evil' in the world highlights the 'good' and 'pure' and vice-versa. Don't get me wrong, there is evil in this world and Justice is a true virtue, but why do people do 'evil' things? I guess that's not for me to answer, but I can give it a shot. Since we are beautiful empty vessels upon Earth, much like the unmolded clay of a potter, the environment is our influence, and our formative years (age 1-7) are basically in the hands of our parents or guardians. This is when the love and nurturing and basic teaching is implemented so that the chilluns can go out into the wild and fulfill their expression in whichever way they please. Let's use a scenario:

A boy and a girl are born into separate families. The boy grew with the influence of both parents and love and discipline were instilled in him. The girl lost her mother to drugs early on and her father needed to fulfill both roles of mother and father, which, naturally, he was unprepared for. The girl was provided love, but no discipline. She was allowed to run off into the wild as she pleased with minimal repercussions and correction. The boy and the girl grow to maturity, are brought together through the cosmic chess game of life, and they are starstruck by each other and fall in love. As they get to know each other and love each other, the boy begins to see the lack of discipline in the girl and is stuck in a predicament. The girl, seeing this as an attack on her free and undisciplined spirit, begins to lash out in cautious defense. The boy can either play 'daddy' and attempt to instill the discipline and guidance that was absent, or to continue in ignorance and watch her spiral into chaos. Since the boy has a good heart and soul, he attempts the first option, which he is slowly annihilated over. The girl ultimately does not know what she wants, and the boy seems to be attracted to her brokenness. Since he was blinded by love and discipline as a child, he couldn't see his parents for what they really were: broken. Just like the girl, just like the boy became through loving her and willingly sacrificing his kindness and love. Now, this boy's vessel has become tainted with a little poison, which he must draw out as willingly as he lets it in. The girl goes along her merry way in ignorance and destruction, until one day, years later, it all hits her at once and she frantically scrambles for where she slipped up, which was always right in front of her, which is what she has decided to fill her vessel with, poison. Poison that has corrupted and broken her vessel over time. End scene.

God help us for we are sinners on this plane, but do we have to be? I don't think so. My best friend Pat would disagree. He thinks that we should lean into our desires and embrace them. This is a beautiful thought, but it is also a quick, one-way road into self-destruction. Pat is broken like the rest of us, but we are all on a path to enlightenment, when attained, comes and goes when needed. My belief is that enlightenment isn't a fixed state that allows one's life to flow easily downstream. On the contrary, enlightenment shines on the dark parts of the soul that bring forth many powerful negative thought-forms that we must address with objectivity, which is not easy. But life isn't easy, as you are aware.

Are we truly social beings? The isolation has me craving human interaction, the touch of a woman, is it all that bad? The devil on my shoulder usually seems to be the most frequent chatterer of the two on my shoulders. This is quite an interesting game we play, perhaps I just don't surround myself with the right people... Interesting. I have become obsessive over a girl that I have projected my feelings and child upon. At the same time, creating a lot of guilt for things of the past and holding onto the most trivial things. By repainting the same continually fading and shifting image of a beautiful, corrupted memory. Amazing, how we can get so zoned onto the pawns and the 'little moves' in this game that we lose sight of the end goal in order to achieve victory. It's also quite funny how we figuratively put a Band-Aid on an internal bleeding wound and convince ourselves that it is healed. This feels like only the beginning of my self-discovery, except the foundation has been reinforced tenfold, which, in turn, lays a clear perspective and framework for the build, my mission. There is a scent in the air right now, like synthetic GMO orange. A sour, citrus smell that is diffusing into the minds of the people, whose realities and 'securities' are drastically changing. We truly are in a grand epoch of growth and change.

We can only bury things for so long, am I wrong? Sometimes it is difficult to locate the fine line between mass paranoia and actual changes in the world that extend beyond individual perspective. Especially in this instant-information age where there is virtually no accountability for these mindless social media posts and these false narratives that are pushed through the multiple forms of media. This has raised some suspicion about Ambassador Azoth, since he has done the genius work of focusing his voice, not on the mass fake media, but on Spitter, the fastest growing social media platform in the world, which no leader in the past has done. I say genius because all of America is on Spitter, losing themselves into a Dopamine trip of likes and 're-spits' where you recycle posts that you like on your profile, Azoth has become quite a trend among the people in this sense and adds more of a 'he's one of us' notion to his persona. In reality, Spitter has been one of the least regulated and propagandized platforms, which the 'shadow' or evil branch of the government have recently started to catch onto.

I think we are all unstable to certain degrees, but is this a fact that should be widely accepted? We tell things to our children in hopes to avoid future pains, but these perceptions shift and distort due to lack of proper nurturing of this half-baked value.

I have also discovered that I have a clinical case of self-sabotage and self-distortion, as in justifying my childhood as something that didn't split along with my parent's divorce at the age of twelve. I never wanted to follow the stereotype of the kid who was destroyed and compromised by a silly divorce, even though this wasn't really within my control. For a part of my split self that craved independence and the desire to become a man, fast. Within the coming months:

- First time I have ever seen my father cry.
- I was informed that my mom was cheating on my dad.
- A new man was moving into my dad's house within a week of the divorce.
- Feeling the need to create a facade for the other kids and adults in my environment (it didn't help that my parents were respected in the community, with my sister and I (Grady hadn't been born yet) being coined as 'model children'.

These were some personal events that naturally came along with time and human nature, which as a kid, is hard to comprehend at eye-level unless experience and transcendence and/or acceptance has occurred. Part of the problem throughout my life has been burying these things as 'non-importants', when they eventually needed to be addressed one way or another. However, I took on the role of therapist way too prematurely, perhaps to understand those emotional burdens while helping others do the same. Pat at one time had asked me, "What about you?" which I would roll my eyes and scoff at, "Me?!" What a silly question! I don't need anyone other than myself! You sir are weak! Transforming into the hard emotion-proof shell and creating this fictional ego that doesn't need help. Quite a mess I have found myself in.

It's easy to think those who love you the most are against you and your ambitions and goals, because they are the ones that deliver the hard truths. Granted, their own projections can come into play, but the balanced and compassionate mind won't allow these distortions to ultimately poison your vessel. I have developed somewhat of a compulsive personality complex during this war in order to cope with certain things. I see pictures and phrases that I feel I must write down or record or else I will lose out on some crucial, life-altering information. Stephen King's words in an interview tend to echo from time to time, "I don't bother to write down every single idea that pops up, the important ones always come back". This form of reassurance has helped relieve some of my internal stress and turmoil.

In addition to my current strife is that I feel that I have no direction, no guide. This isn't true, of course, but a learning and unmatured mind can easily become bitter when it doesn't truly know what it wants, just raw frustration needing to be transformed within me. Our parents will attempt to give the best advice that they can, but WE are ultimately the ones that must make the decisions. It took me a bad break-up and a trip to jail in order to accept counsel from family and a therapist. Even as I sit here, my motivation dwindles. It feels like I long for an audience and acceptance, but I know it is not what I need. I accept that there are loving and divine energies at play for all of us, not just me. I accept that I have been gifted with this experience and this lifetime in order to help usher in and inspire unconditional love and self-awareness.

March 21st (Spring Equinox)

People have gathered from near and far to see Ambassador Azoth speak regarding the corruption in our government and the true story behind the 'Blackouts'. The shadow government has tried very hard to disrupt Azoth's communication with the People through paid-off terror groups that cause violence and noise in order to paint Azoth's following as 'radicals' and 'domestic terrorists'. However, at this point, the People know better. Thousands of people, from all colors and backgrounds, united in the name of Liberty and Peace and to end corruption with their unified song. At the front of the movement, stood Ambassador Alexander Azoth, with his eagle-like stare, standing at the podium. In the center front-panel of the shiny oak of the podium, a gold emblazoned emblem was engraved. A simple, cartoonish symbol that Azoth used as an emblem for Peace and Fertility: A Hass Avocado.

At the end of the Ambassador's speech, the crowd in a perpetual uproar, he concluded with, "I would like to read a poem passed down through my family that I have kept for a crucial time like this". Azoth pulled out a browned, leathery piece of paper that had survived for this moment:

Die Avocado (translated from German)

In the Cold, she will not grow

Only in the nurturing warmth she will show

The rich fertility of Life and Love

Fresh, green oil that soothes the soul.

When we toil, head in the soil, we gaze up at the setting sun

For the battle has been fought, the battle has been won

Take my hand, as we journey through the sands of time

Through the Darkness we ride, Heaven and Hell coincide

With the grace of the Mother and Father

We stand for Truth and Love

Find the warm, nurturing climate within your soul

and let your avocado tree grow

So that the world can see why, the Light cannot die

Lost souls can only cover, obscure, in hopes that the rest will

forget.

But fear not, my child

Do not go numb

For the golden hour is yet to come.

(Ende)

God Bless us and no matter what happens, I love you all,

unconditionally.

End, for now...

"Each nation has its own ray in that great source of light that
we see, that is the sun". -Nikola Tesla (*Everything is Light)*

The Poet

A moody child and wildly wise

Pursued the game with joyful eyes,

Which chose, like meteors, their way,

And rived the dark with private ray.

They overleapt the horizon's edge,

Searched with Apollo's privilege, through man, and woman,

and sea, and star.

Saw the dance of nature forward far.

Through worlds, and races, and terms, and times

Saw musical order, and painting rhymes.

Olympian bards who sung Divine ideas below,

Which always finds us young

And always keeps us so.

-Ralph Waldo Emerson

The Call to Wisdom

'*Wisdom cries aloud in the street, in the markets she raises her*

voice; at the head of the noisy streets, she cries out; at the

entrance of the city gates she speaks;

"How long, O simple ones, will you love being simple? How

long will scoffers delight in their scoffing and fools hate

knowledge? If you turn at my reproof, behold, I will pour out

my spirit to you. I will make my words known to you. Because I

have called you and you refused to listen, have stretched out my

hand and no one has heeded, because you have ignored all my

counsel and would have none of my reproof, I also will laugh at

your calamity; I will mock when terror strikes you, when terror

strikes you like a storm and your calamity comes like a

whirlwind, when distress and anguish come upon you. Then

they will call upon me, but I will not answer; they will seek me

diligently but will not find me. Because they hated knowledge

and did not choose the fear of the Lord, would have none of my

counsel and despised all my reproof, therefore they shall eat

the fruit of their way, and have their fill of their own devices.

For the simple are killed by their turning away, and the

complacency of fools destroys them, but whoever listens to me

will dwell secure and will be at ease, without dread of

disaster."' -Proverbs 1:20-33

"Set aside all meritorious deeds and religious rituals, and just

surrender completely to my will with firm faith and loving

devotion. I shall liberate you from all sins, the bonds of karma.

Do not grieve." -Bhagavad Gita 18.66

"We cannot change the world; we can change only the lives of

a few sincere souls whose time for change has come by His

grace." -Bhagavad Gita

Zeal's Journal:

(03/21/17)

Squeeze into the frame

Disregard the fame

Duck to dodge the shameful blame

You know the story, what is this game?

Who is the Patron?

Scramble for liberation & information

Call tomorrow received, higher calling

Sweet Surrender

Down with the bloody red sickness, Up with the Good

We came for this, don't get stuck

Decompression

Release

-Z

(2/11/19)

All seek opportunity, this is a serious game

Those who seek it as it is

What is? We can't be sure…

Faith? Wraith? Words can be used dichotomously

Bi-partisan anomaly

The lights flood in without voice, illuminating all that is hidden

Tripped up pharaohs sleeping in their tombs

Remaining faithful to the tunes

Human bonds within the square

We asked and we were given this chance.

-Z

(12/25/15)

Trinity. Infinity. Sublimity

Reach in and grab at your Will

Some may bite, some may hide, yet they all smile

Invitingly

We have to discern with the Holy Eye, given by God.

Described in the Word

Do not listen to their lies, no matter how seemingly innocent,

sweet, or sly

We are one, but the message has been distorted

Surly Scribe, hearken closely.

You will come to stand.

-Z

12/08/15 The Journey

There are times in life

When one must stop

In order to realize the scum and the slop,

To find inside, what lies beneath

Remove the sword, from within its sheath

You hold the key

As you soon shall see

How vibrant you can truly be

Your time will come, with the rising sun

Our journey has just begun

-z

12/08/15- The Way she Lies

She eats

She sleeps

She laughs

She weeps

Her pale skin against the sheets

She runs

She leaps

Frantic for the things she seeks

She is the wolf

...and I am the sheep

-Z

(07/07/19)-

Today is the mark of a new era for me. Age is irrelevant, time is

over. It's up to us now to put a stop to the evil that has been

upon us like a sickness for a while now. It's grind-time. furreal.

I won't let myself slip back into darkness, ignorance, denial. It

is so liberating to put your heart in the hands of Jesus, bless his

name. I have always been in such strong denial of the truth

because it's a hard pill to swallow, especially if the darkness

has been guiding you, but that's the whole point of maturing I

guess; to accept the truth with a smile and admire the

challenge. I can feel that things are going to get a whole lot

worse. It's been too quiet. I've had time to decide. I've been

given many chances and I have learned many things in my 22

years. How much time we waste trying to create and maintain

our bubbles of comfort, gripping them so tight that they pop. I

am a soldier of God and Jesus and am willing to do anything in the glory and love of His name and the salvation of Good. Evil

doesn't stand a chance. We will all be ready.

__August 14th, 2019:__ It's very important for me to remain

vigilant and aware to maintain and stabilize this granted

awareness that I constantly get into the habit of taking

advantage of. I've been slacking on my journaling, growing

lazy and tired. As the tide flows into the shore, it must also

retreat. I woke up with a feeling of wrongdoing towards others

and wondered how I've been betrayed by those who I 'love

most'. Ignorance is bliss, but it is also a guaranteed way to

never break free from the programming. There are going to be

big decisions that I have to make, and questions that will

continue to eat me alive; are we supposed to love? Obviously,

but why is it obvious? Am I on the right path? Am I even on a

path? I guess there is no right path since energy just re-

circulates and changes form... How do I break free from

harmful relationships? How can we identify if they are

harmful? I feel like we know the answers to each of these

questions, but can we accept the truth behind them? I have

blatantly done wrong things just to cross them off of my bucket

list. Pitiful conditions, flying too close to the sun, for I am

Icarus. Much love. Stay tuned.

__August 6th-__ I am having trouble falling asleep, which hasn't been a problem since I have been freed from probation which has been about a year now, I have been experimenting with my mind and body, going in and out of different chemical love affairs, and building myself each time I enter these fluctuations, changing something every time, or at least trying to. It is a very interesting time we are living in; things don't feel like they used to. I'm 22 years old but it feels like I have lived for a lot longer. I have an affinity for classical music, tobacco, and traditional outlooks on things that I find so attractive and aesthetic for some strange reason. My ideal world has a classic feel with a modern splash of technology and design. I'm stuck in the crevice between not caring about anything and letting God guide me to whatever corner I am blown to, or abiding by the rules and mastering this material world as well as my thoughts and actions. I keep telling myself that NOW I will change, NOW I will create a business in a week or two. We live in a time of ignorance and frustration, complacent. I have been drawn to finding movies that have a parallel or synonymous take on what society is experiencing. I like the movie 'Wall-E' a lot because it shows the people as fat and governed by the robotic AI technology that was created to regulate and operate the ship so that the people can become fat and atrophied. Earth has become a wasteland so the world lives on this enormous ship in outer space that can simulate a world of its own. It is *amazing how compounded brainwashing can go both ways; we can rewrite our programs to inspire growth and love, or we can allow fear and negativity to rule our worlds. I am beginning to see that things are both more simple and more complex than we are led to believe. I have been searching tirelessly for that 'magic answer', that one word or bit of information in a book that will somehow blow the lid off this whole operation and take me into the 4th dimension, but we seem to have a mission here and now on this Earth. I am fortunate enough to see this and be aware of this, a day-to-day struggle with fear and complacency. I hold onto these people and systems that have become a part of me, I have been going through a long period of breaking and rebuilding. This stage in my life is going to prove that my destiny has always been guiding me in the right direction, it seems to be about the journey and the tests.*

Intuitive Writing, Take One:

There are times when you must smile, there are times to be serious. it is possible to be done all at once, but tread carefully, they're watching. The power is always within, it doesn't have to be something extraordinary, sometimes you can't see your own light (dark or bright) but others can. You are here to show more people what life can actually mean to them within the divine blueprint. If you really want to help people find their strengths, you must find your own. Start from the beginning, work your way to now, you already know you can write, classical music can serve as a catalyst, this is good, not cliche. You will rise, you will fall, like the tides of the ocean you are, let the energy flow in and interpret with your heart with no comparison to others, feel it burning in your belly, that feeling which you confuse for sexual excitement. Be careful where you choose to spend your energy and focus. **Why am I so in love with art and entertainment that represent character development?** *That's just it, the development. There are those who understand earlier than others, the reason for this is to teach what you have been given, to impact the world. A heart to serve and to love will continue to serve and love, you are a survivor, a winter soldier, a healer, a writer, a sun of God. You will get to where you want to be, maybe you're already there (:*

What should I do next? *Flow through your heart and not as much through your head, the right brain is connected to the heart, hence the left brain is set to logic and fundamentals. Do nothing, do everything, just keep in mind, that without Love and Compassion, we are just programs in the matrix. You will be fine.*

November 4th: There is a sickness in the world, an ignorant ailment that seems to be woven into our DNA. Everything seems to be so predictable except my own thoughts and behavior. It's funny how it all works, I can't let this discourage me. I look up at the sun from the belly of the beast with tired eyes, as if I experienced death countless times. I am not sure how long I will last; the walls seem to close in during times like these... I find myself alone with my pen and paper and ocean of thoughts and emotions. I am trying to solve this big puzzle, like the answers haven't been in front of me the whole time. My biggest ailments: the delusion of holding onto thinking that Calysta and I still love each other and that she is my 'soulmate', making the wrong choices and becoming irreparably damaged, becoming poor and poverty-stricken, never finding my true community. Now, time for strengths: A heart to serve, a vision of greatness, ability to see and say things as they are and being able to shift perspectives. My mission seems to be to elevate others as I elevate myself. To overcome lust, anger, fear, and replace them with the infinite source of love. It's hard to do this within the system that we are bound to, but that's the battle. Times are changing and so are the people, we can either treat this time of change as a threat or embrace it as our natural evolution. It is very easy to be deceived during this age of deception, for this we were granted divine discernment which, in form, is realization of the higher self, where nothing can confuse you from who you really are and are meant to be. I want to help people find their true selves; do I need to find myself first? The needle seems to be fluttering over 'yes'. It's hard to change, but as time goes on, I realize how necessary these changes are for my survival and growth. I will be patiently waiting with a smile (:

November 22nd: 'Lonely'

I was at work today (customer service agent for a pharmaceutical company) sitting in front of my computer. Two cups of coffee deep and a head full of caffeinated thoughts racing around through my prefrontal cortex. The high energy of a Friday in a corporate office setting is quite legendary; you see employees who were walking zombies Monday through Thursday become almost too happy on Friday, for it to come back to the beginning of the brutal cycle. I was thinking about this girl that I had been seeing once in a blue moon, here and there, who was such a pocketful of sunshine, a beautiful soul. She has a boyfriend and I've been a good boy, not trying to cause any wreckages. It's interesting having been trained to care so much about physique and reputation in a courtship, shifting my values as I get older and more mature causes me to look for a lot more in a girl. This weird feeling has stuck with me with certain women, the melting feeling of complete surrender and submission as our souls merge together in a spiritual and energetic dance. I instinctively want to fight this feeling... I have let it get the best of me too many times, yet I keep running into it head on. I guess we'll see how things pan out, it's funny when we get to that point where we just don't care what other people think anymore and that's when the magic happens. Much love, Stay tuned.

December 20th: 'Bound'- *Throughout reading the Bhagavad-Gita (Sacred Song), I have had the fortunate pleasure of tying many loose ends I had with modern religious institutions and standard ideology in general. For example, the fact that we cannot grasp the infinite is mentioned almost immediately within the text. A lot of Christian and Catholic sects use God personified as a man or force that is not omnipresent in all things. Something that also resonated deeply with me was the karmic bonds that we form throughout lifetimes and how these vices pop up time and time again in order for us to deal with these karmic bonds, cutting them with the sword of self-knowledge. I have found myself creating some powerful bonds myself for the desperate attempt to feel connected to people and things. That little split-second of foresight before one decides can either be ignored, or it can be trusted. Mostly ignored. My bonds are that of lust, passion, and corruption. These bonds keep me awake at night sometimes. I wish to eliminate them.*

***December 26th, 'Confession'-** It appears I have emerged from a dark, murky water that forced me to bathe in self-pity and self-loathing. This Christmas was pivotal, as I grow deeper into myself and my spiritual journey. It's interesting how we think we are doing so well and then get a nice humbling smack on the bottom. Astro-theology has been a major doorway into my self-understanding, which I feel is one of the primary goals of this science. However, I have unwittingly plunged myself into the biggest rabbit-hole I have encountered. Analyzing the self from an objective standpoint is easier written than done, so this is where I seem to slip up, for one of my vices is self-criticism and the 'talking down' of the self which I commonly place under the guise of 'humility'. Once we accept ourselves for who we are; imperfect beings striving for perfection, there is a true humility that gives us a foundation to build upon. I instantly became swept away by Astrology and how this science ties together many loose ends. I subconsciously start to 'act out' and try to fulfill my astrological signature, now that I have the knowledge. With me being a Capricorn sun, I decided to feed these energies and capitalize them in order to become a True Archetypal representation of the 10th sign of the zodiac. Structure, ruled by Saturn, dark, winter, formidable. This took the attention away from listening and brought forth a new form of fulfilling, putting on another mask, only this was a more evolved mask. Something that many therapists and* *psychologists keep a secret, or possibly deny altogether, is that everyone has the power to become their own therapist, with our strengthened faith and counsel in God. Who would need therapy if they could solve their own problems? This is something that Carl Jung seemed to seek; addressing the root cause of the mental unbalance rather than simply treat with medications and provide watered-down time-killing responses. I have shut myself in due to fear of myself, fear of lust, anger. I have seemingly an insatiable desire for knowledge, but I have disregarded wisdom, the soaking in of truth and knowledge. A power that I have yet to understand. This is paramount to the rest right now. Maybe because I like it that way. There is a force behind the pen, it seems dark, but what is dark? Is this my mission? Explore the darkness, you will find light.*

February 24th: *Things have been changing rapidly over the past few months. People are waking up at a rate that is astonishing, it seems like people are slowly beginning to realize what is happening around us, right before our eyes, and that is a mass shift in our consciousness as we have proven that we are ready for the ultimate test. I feel confident that this test is the battle between our lower and higher natures: the creative mind versus the logical mind. Or is it war?*

I am protected by the leaves

Sheltered by the trees

Giving a shoulder for her to cry

I'm not the guy

But something came over me

A warm surge of energy

Where the only thing that mattered was curing her sadness

To make her smile.